ALL I WANT IS YOU

CASSIE CROSS

ALL I WANT
is You

CASSIE CROSS

ALSO BY CASSIE CROSS

Standalone Titles:

Meeting Mr. Wright

Kiss Me At Midnight

Series:

The Dirty Little Series:

Dirty Little Secrets

Dirty Little Lies

The Billionaire's Desire Series:

The Billionaire's Desire

The Billionaire's Christmas

The Billionaire's Best Friend

Quickies Series:

The Quickies Collection: Volume 1

CHAPTER
One

It's been four months since I graduated from the University of Virginia, crammed everything I owned into the trunk of my Honda, and headed north for a new life and a new job here in Washington, D.C.

Working as a junior associate at a mid-level accounting firm isn't exactly my dream job, but it pays the rent.

The city is as bustling and intimidating as it is beautiful, but I'm having trouble connecting with new people. My best friend Alexa lives nearby, but she works long hours and isn't around all that much. My other friends from school are scattered throughout the country, either at new jobs in new cities like me, or back at home with their parents.

So, in the absence of any kind of social life, I've formed a deep, lasting relationship with Netflix. Occasionally I spice things up with a pint of mint chip, whenever I'm compelled to eat my feelings. This is pretty much my new normal, and tonight? Alexa's had enough. She's staging an intervention.

"Are you gonna get ready, or are you just gonna lie there?" Alexa yells from somewhere in the recesses of my bedroom closet.

Snuggling the fluffiest pillow I own, I burrow down deep into my comfy mattress and turn up the volume on my television. "Just gonna lie here."

"*C'mon!*" Alexa throws a balled-up T-shirt across the room, which lands right on my ass. "I need you to pick a dress."

Alexa holds the only two little black dresses that I own, ones I rarely wear because I *hate* going to the kinds of places I'd have to wear them. Like the one Alexa is intent on dragging me to tonight.

"Short or shorter?" With a hanger in each hand, Alexa displays my options. "The short one accentuates your curves, but the shorter one says, 'I'm here to have sex tonight.'"

"Maybe *you* should wear that one then."

Alexa sighs, tosses my dresses on the bed, then walks over and pries the remote from my hand. She aims it at the television, and a second later the screen flickers off.

"Why did you do that?" I'm not proud of the mild panic that laces its way through my words.

"I'm instigating a breakup between you and your boyfriend, Netflix."

My comforter pools around my hips as I sit up, indignant. "Our relationship is totally healthy, okay? It makes binge-watching so *easy.*"

With an exasperated sigh, Alexa sits down on the edge of the bed. "Stop deflecting."

I consider arguing with her, but I press my lips together to stop myself from speaking. I don't want to fight. "Okay."

"You've gotta get out and meet some new people. You need to stop hiding and let yourself have some fun. The way things are now, you're going to wake up one morning when you're fifty and regret the fact that the only meaningful relationship you have is with your television."

"To be fair, televisions will probably be obsolete 27 years from now."

Alexa narrows her eyes. *"Hayley."*

Having a person in your life who knows you better than anyone else is really great, except for when they call you out on your shit when you're not ready to be called out on it.

"I'm fine with my life the way it is," I lie.

Alexa gives me a look that screams *you've got to be kidding me*. "Weren't you just complaining about your dry spell, like, two days ago?"

I glare at her. "Using my involuntary celibacy against me is just rude." She's right, though. I *was* just complaining about it. I'm at the point now where I feel like there should be a sign above my bed that reads:

DAYS SINCE NON-SOLO ORGASM:
186

Not that I'm keeping track or anything.

"No-strings-attached fun awaits you if you just put on one of these dresses."

"I hate clubs," I counter, which is the absolute well-documented truth. "Can't I just put on my favorite jeans, go to the grocery store, and...I don't know, meet someone in the produce section?"

Alexa lets out a sharp laugh. "I think you're missing the point of a one-night stand, sweetie. You want to find someone dirty-hot and dangerous who can make you come 20 times and doesn't care if you call him back. Your little produce section fantasy is marriage material. If that's what you're looking for, then a club is definitely the wrong place to go."

"You know I'm not looking for..." I narrow my eyes and lower my voice. "The *M*-word."

"Never in my life have I met a commitment-phobe who turns up her nose at the idea of casual sex," Alexa replies, rolling her eyes. "You have a problem, and I'm offering you a solution. Plus...free drinks."

"It's not the casual sex I'm turning up my nose at. I *want* the casual sex. It's the going to a club part of this scenario that I dislike. It was so easy in college...guys were always so ready and willing, and they were *everywhere*. All I had to do was step foot out of my dorm and I'd practically trip over two guys who were anxious to get into my pants."

Alexa laughs. "There are tons of guys around who are anxious to get into your pants," she assures me. "You just have to go outside a ten-foot radius to find them now."

"Tell me about it."

"You look hot in those dresses, Hayley," Alexa says, nodding toward where they lie at the foot of my bed. "I'd be willing to bet that you won't even have to stay at the club for very long."

That gets a smile out of me. Apparently, a little bit of flattery goes a long way for me these days.

"It'll be fun," Alexa continues, knowing that she's managed to put a dent in my defenses. "At the very least you'll get to spend some time in the land of the living."

"Hey," I reply, offended. "I go out in the land of the living all the time."

"Yeah," she snorts. "To go to work, get more ice cream, and then come home."

That one stings a bit, and Alexa must notice because her expression immediately softens.

"Look, I know you're having a hard time. It was the same way for me when I moved up here last year, but you're not making it any easier on yourself."

She has a point. I hate it when she has a point. It's one night...what can it hurt?

With a deeply aggrieved sigh, I swing my legs over the side of the bed and stand. Alexa looks up at me with a hint of a smile and a little bit of hope in her eyes.

"Hand me a dress."

"Which one? Short or shorter?"

If I'm going, might as well go all the way. "Shorter."

"Is this as awful as you thought it'd be?" Alexa asks.

I don't answer, because really...it's worse.

The club's bass is pumping, the smell of sweat and too much alcohol in the air. A sea of bodies moves along to the beat on the dance floor, while Alexa and I fight for a little bit of real estate at the bar.

A guy slides up behind me, pressing his cold glass against the sliver of exposed skin at the small of my back as he grinds his erection against my ass, his free hand inching dangerously low across my belly. His cologne is as strong as his advances, and I shudder when he leans in close, his hot breath on my ear.

Gross.

"No thanks," I say firmly, pinching his wrist to get his hand off of me as I jam my stiletto into his foot as hard as I can.

"*Bitch*." He gives up easily, though, flashing an annoyed

look in my direction before he slinks back into the crowd, moving on to less fortunate prey.

Men like these are the reason I hate clubs, assuming any woman is willing and there for the taking, available to touch however he wants. I realize this is basically a meat market, but I'd like someone to understand that there are boundaries, and give me the chance to indicate I'm willing to have mine crossed before they do the crossing.

Alexa's busy trying to find some commitment-free fun of her own, but by the looks of it, she's having about as much luck as I am. She twists away from a handsy jerk a few feet away and makes her way back to my side.

"Remind me why we're here again?" I ask Alexa, before taking a sip of my whiskey sour. It was free, which seems to be the only redeeming quality of this shitty evening so far.

"We're here to get you laid!" she replies with an enthusiastic yell, and her words reverberate through the crowd.

Everyone in our immediate vicinity stares at us.

Oh god. Have I mentioned that I *hate* clubs?

"She isn't interested in any of you!" Alexa shouts as the music picks up again, then she grabs my hand and leads me away from the bar. "I'm so sorry about that. I was just trying to make sure you could hear me over the music."

Alexa looks so upset with herself that I can't possibly be angry with her. She only has my libido's best interest at heart.

"It's okay," I assure her; even though my cheeks feel hot as the sun from sheer embarrassment as we push our way through the crowd.

"Wanna leave?"

All I'd have to do is nod and this failed experiment of an evening would be blessedly over. I should tell her yes; part of me really wants to. But for reasons that even I don't fully understand, I say, "No."

We're a few drinks in, and Alexa's off grinding against some man who looks like he's old enough to be her father. She seems happy, so I can't hate her for that, but I *can* hate her for leaving me here alone.

Just me and my drink all by ourselves in the corner like a couple of losers. I'm trying to convince myself to stop being such a wallflower and *dance* already. I toss back what's left in my glass and set it on the ledge behind me when an astonishingly, unbelievably hot guy catches my eye.

Actually, *astonishingly, unbelievably hot* doesn't even begin to accurately describe this man.

Hot Guy is incredibly tall, has a mop of dirty-blond hair, and raspy scruff peppering his movie-star jawline. A tight henley shows off every inch of his broad chest and muscular arms from where he stands across the room, just *staring* at me.

Seems I've caught his eye, too. That *never* happens to me.

His lips part when our eyes meet, like he wants to call out to me or something, but instead he keeps on staring. Staring in a way that makes my heart beat double time, that makes my knees weak. He doesn't smile, doesn't nod, doesn't do anything other than look at me like he wants to *devour* me.

Without really thinking, I hurriedly make my way over, not even trying to play it cool. I slide between couples who are bumping and grinding on the dance floor, and when I reach Hot Guy, he smiles. It's not the slick grin of a slime ball who knows he's going to get laid tonight; it's sweet and sexy, with just the hint of a dimple shining through.

"Hi," he says, all soft and familiar despite the fact that we're complete strangers.

"Hi."

"I'm glad you came over." He leans in close, and all I can

think about is how *good* he smells. I want to press my face into his neck and breathe deep. I want his tongue to become familiar with every single inch of my body.

I'm feeling turned on and brazen, and the way Hot Guy's eyes skate across my body makes me pretty confident that he feels the same way, too. That's what gives me the courage to say, "You don't seem like the kind of guy who has difficulty making women come."

I certainly hope not, at least.

Hot Guy lets out a shocked laugh, and his hazel eyes darken with something that looks a lot like lust. His hands find their way to the small of my back and he gives me a gentle tug, pulling me closer to him and away from the crowd.

"I'm not," he replies, his scruff rasping against my skin as his lips brush the shell of my ear. "I can show you if you'd like." His voice is low and rumbly; it gives me goose bumps all over.

I'd like that. Very much. I nod as my hand slips across his chest, over the solid, defined muscle underneath his soft cotton shirt.

"What's your name?"

"Hunter," he replies.

I turn my head and inhale, memorizing his scent as he pulls me closer. Even though I don't feel threatened at all, there's a comforting kind of safety in his arms that I hadn't anticipated. The moment is perfect; I pretty much forget that we aren't the only two people in the room.

Then Hunter's muscles tighten beneath my hands, and his entire body tenses.

A spike of fear rushes through me, making my heart tap frantically against my breastbone, spreading a tingling rush out to my fingertips.

"Hayley," he says soothingly.

But there's nothing soothing about it, because I'm positive I didn't tell him my name.

"I need you to trust me, okay?" Hunter's eyes meet mine for one intense, drawn-out moment before his gaze flits back to the crowd. "Do as I say."

Gunshots ring out before I have a chance to answer.

Hunter has me on the floor in the blink of an eye, my stomach pressed against the cold, unforgiving concrete as pieces of drywall rain down around me. He covers me like a blanket, cradling me against his chest, using his body to keep me safe. His hand shields my face from the falling debris, and the only thing that keeps me from screaming is his steady voice in my ear.

"I've got you," he tells me. "It's gonna be okay."

I'm not sure why I believe him.

The gunshots stop abruptly and the guns clatter to the floor. The sickening thump of fists striking bodies fill the air as Hunter picks me up and ushers me out of the room, his body curled around mine, protecting me from any remaining danger.

In the chaos, I manage to catch a glimpse of Alexa. A burly guy is curled around her much like Hunter is curled around me.

I'm about to thank Hunter when he pulls me behind a curtain, between some A/V equipment and the club's service entrance.

"C'mon." He tugs my hand. "We don't have a lot of time."

I can't help but scoff in spite of my gratitude. "I appreciate you saving my life back there, so don't get me wrong, but why on earth would I go anywhere with you when someone was just *shooting at you*?"

Hunter's face softens, all the urgency gone as he reaches up and cups my cheek.

"Hayley," he says urgently. "They weren't shooting at me. They were shooting at *you*."

CHAPTER Two

Hayley looks at me the way most of my clients do when the reality of their situation hits them: confusion mixed with a flash of terror. She's living in a world where someone wants to hurt her, and everyone, everything is a potential threat.

It'll be awhile before she feels completely safe again.

My clients usually have a few days or weeks to come to terms with this kind of situation. Some need general security, some need help with a specific threat. There's almost always warning, time for strategic planning. Time for acceptance.

Hayley has all of 30 seconds.

Wasting time flirting with her didn't help. I lost control

of myself like a damned teenager, like we had all the time in the world. I knew what she looked like—I had seen a few pictures—but seeing her in person, I *wanted* her in a way that I haven't wanted someone in a long time. The wavy blonde hair flowing over her shoulder, those full, pink lips, that dress that hugged her body. All of it drew me in.

I liked her attention, liked that she zeroed in on me in a crowded room. That she felt the same connection I did.

That connection made me lose sight of the whole mission. *I* put her in more danger.

It's a glaring reminder of why I *never* date clients.

Not that Hayley is a typical client.

"Someone was shooting at me," she says, sounding more confused than panicked, trying to work out what I just told her. "Why? Who would even…"

I wrap my hand around her wrist, moving toward the service entrance door, the beginning of my hastily planned escape route.

"I don't have time to explain right now," I tell her, giving her a gentle tug. "We'll talk when you're safe."

"The people who were shooting at me just became intimately familiar with some fists," she replies, hooking her thumb back toward the club's main room. "I think I'm safe. Besides, I can't leave Alexa here, and we need to wait for the police. They're going to have some questions about what happened here tonight."

I want to pick her up and carry her out of the building. Knowing that it'll be easier to disappear if we don't draw any attention to ourselves is the only thing that stops me.

"You have to come with me, Hayley." I admire her concern for her friend, but I'm desperate to make her see reason. I haven't lost a client yet—she's not going to be the first. "One of my guys is taking care of Alexa. He's gonna keep her safe, and I have another one here to deal with the police. They're—"

"Excuse me, your *guys?*"

"I'm a bodyguard."

"You're a bodyguard," she repeats, sliding her hand up into her hair, pulling it away from her face. She scrunches her brows together, giving me a look. I just made myself a human shield to keep her from getting shot; I'm not sure what I can do or say in the next few seconds that will make her trust me.

"Do you remember Carson Taylor?" I ask.

Mentioning his name lands like a physical blow. Hayley flinches like I've slapped her. I know she remembers him. Carson told me the horror story that was their breakup, the way he treated her before and after.

I've seen the restraining order.

I know first hand that Carson leaves a hell of an aftermath that's difficult to navigate.

"I remember him." Hayley squares her shoulders. She raises her chin, defiant, but the tremble in her voice betrays her.

"He got himself in trouble with some bad people," I tell her, which is an understatement. He owes a crime lord a shitload of money, and that guy wants to take the one thing he thinks Carson still cares about—Hayley—to persuade him to pay up. But you can't bleed a rock, and I'm not letting Carson's bad decisions hurt anyone else. "He knew they'd come after you to get to him, and they have. I can't protect you if I don't get you out of here."

Hayley bites her lip. She wants to believe me. "Alexa is my best friend. My family. I can't just—"

"I know that trusting me is a lot to ask. We just met, and this isn't the way I wanted to introduce myself to you." I recall what she said when we met a few minutes ago, what those words did to me. What they made me want to do to her. I push all that away, making myself focus on her safety and nothing else. "Alexa is in good hands, I promise. If you want to keep her and everyone else in this club safe, we have to get out of here. Now."

Hayley nods. I carefully open the service entrance door and poke my head out, unsure of what waits on the other side.

The coast is clear, just as I'd hoped.

I take Hayley's hand and we step outside.

"You don't have a getaway car?" Hayley asks quietly, the first time she's spoken in the past five minutes.

We're a few blocks away from the club, and I haven't seen any signs of trouble. I glance back at her as I lead her through the last of countless alleyways, toward Dupont Circle. The evening crowd is in full swing, and it'll be easy for us to disappear.

"I don't like being in a car in the busy parts of the city," I explain. "If we hit any kind of traffic, we're sitting ducks."

We pass the back entrance to a greasy Chinese takeout spot, and I pluck a jacket off the railing, then slip it over her shoulders.

"It's mine," I tell her. I'd left it here when I did a quick run-through of our escape route right before I showed up at the club. If I'd been even a *minute* later...

Hayley slides her arms through the sleeves, completely swimming in the leather. She nestles her head against the collar, closing her eyes as she breathes deep. The smell must comfort her, and that thought makes me want to kiss her until she forgets her own name.

I shake my head a little, like that'll get my mind off her. I've got to *focus*.

I wrap my arm around Hayley and tuck her against my side, walking at a pace that's brisk enough to weave through the crowd, but nothing that'll draw attention.

"Let your hair fall down around your face," I tell her, like we're having a casual conversation. "Tug the jacket closed so no one can see your dress. The less identifiable you are, the better."

She does as I say.

The goal is to pass ourselves off as any other couple, like I gave her my jacket to keep out the unseasonable chill in the air. We continue for a couple of blocks, then take a detour onto a residential street. Leaves are rustling in the wind; I have to concentrate to make out any suspicious sounds.

Hayley's whole frame is stiff and on guard, so I rub her shoulder, and she relaxes against me.

Apart from another couple about a hundred feet or so ahead of us, there doesn't appear to be anyone else around. Going down Swann on our way to 17th seems to have been a good choice. I keep my arm around Hayley, partly for the ruse, and partly for comfort. We're close to the rendezvous point when I catch the quick clip of footsteps behind us.

"Laugh," I tell Hayley. "Laugh like I said something funny."

She lets out a noise that sounds a lot like a dying cat, and I can't help but smile. I twirl her into an alleyway to our left, and her surprised laugh that follows seems genuine. I plant my hand against the wall next to Hayley's face to keep her hidden and press my body against hers. It's strategic; it keeps her protected if I'm going to have to deal with the person behind us, and makes us look like a horny couple taking a minute to ourselves if I don't.

Her breasts press against my chest with every breath she takes, and I have to actively ignore the fact that I'm a man to focus on being a bodyguard. It's difficult with Hayley, though, everything about her draws me in. She's so gorgeous. Tousled blonde hair and clear blue eyes with a smile that lights up a room. I slide my thumb along the plump curve of her lower lip, briefly wondering what she tastes like.

The footsteps echo closer.

I press my forehead to Hayley's, turn my head to the side just enough to get a good look at the woman passing by, heels clicking heavily on the sidewalk. She doesn't even notice us here.

"Why did you do that?" Hayley asks, her voice trembling.

I don't know what she's asking. There are a few things I've done in the past minute that require explanation, so I go for the simplest answer.

"I wanted to get out of the way," I explain. "I don't like having anyone on my six." The tip of my nose brushes against hers as I turn my head and face her. The air between us is charged. I could lean in and—

"What's a six?"

I let out a quick huff of a laugh, effectively breaking the moment.

Hayley's eyebrows bunch together irritably. "You don't have to laugh at me, I just—"

"I'm not laughing at you," I tell her, reaching up and tucking a strand of hair behind her ear. "You are a surprise, Hayley Grey."

The alarm on my watch chirps—we're already running late to get the car. "Come on." I push away from the wall and reach for Hayley's hand. "We've got to get out of here."

At the corner of Willard and 17th, one of my best employees

leans on an unassuming tan sedan in front of the red row house we'd designated as a meeting point.

Davis is a big guy, intimidating. Hayley hangs back on the sidewalk as I approach him. "Inconspicuous," he says, nodding toward the car as he tosses me a set of keys. "Just like you wanted, Boss."

"Thanks. Are we clear?" No one followed us, and I want to make sure no one followed him, either.

Davis nods. "All clear." He looks over at Hayley, whose hands are twisted into the lapel of my jacket. She looks nervous, and I don't blame her. It's one thing to ask her to walk with me to safety, it's another thing to ask her to get in a car to places unknown.

I know I'm asking a lot, but the stakes are high.

"She okay?"

I nod. "Shaken up."

Davis presses his lips together, then gives me a wary look. "You sure you wanna do this? One of the other guys can handle it. You know we're capable."

He knows I'm too close to this. Hell, I know it too, but that's not stopping me. I tell him what I told him earlier, when he asked me the same thing. "I need to take care of this one myself."

He nods; he knew that'd be my answer. "Darcy packed a bag for her. I put it in the trunk along with a cooler with enough food for the next couple of days."

"Thanks."

Davis has connections and ways of making criminals back off. The guy who's after Carson—Damien Hunt—has some skeletons in his closet that Davis is gonna bring into the light of day if Damien doesn't agree to forget Hayley exists. Davis is the only man for this job; he knows how to finesse a situation, and he's a powerful negotiator.

I'm more of a fan of brute force, and the situation with Hayley is far too delicate for that.

"You'll let me know when you've taken care of the problem?" I ask.

"The hot second. And I'll let you know when Garrett's done with Carson."

Davis and I shake on it, and he takes off as I walk over and open the door for Hayley.

"C'mon," I say, giving her an encouraging smile. "Get in."

She does not get in. Even though she's still fidgeting with my jacket, she gives me a defiant look. It's annoying as all hell given the circumstances, but admiration manages to break its way through.

"We don't have time for this," I tell her, impatiently casing the area. The longer we stand around, the greater chance we have of our streak of good luck ending, and I want to get out of here *now*. "I can't keep you safe if you don't trust me."

She looks around, bouncing on the heels of her feet. Her resistance is crumbling.

"It's just gonna be you and me," I tell her. "No one knows where we're headed, and no one will follow us. Everything's gonna be okay, but we have to go now."

She hesitates a second longer, then lowers herself into the car.

CHAPTER
Three

"Do you remember Carson Taylor?"

Hunter's words replay on a loop in my head as we drive along a lonely two-lane road. How could I possibly forget him? My first serious boyfriend, the charismatic guy everyone I loved warned me of, the troubled person who drifted further and further away from me the harder I tried to hold on to him.

He stole from me and lied to me to chase a high. That he's in trouble with bad people doesn't surprise me. That they think they can come after me to get to him absolutely does.

Carson and I had an instant, deep connection that left a trail of destruction in its wake. One he never seemed to get over, and one I've spent the last year and a half trying to forget.

We were a cautionary tale, a warning against falling hard and fast, of acting on impulse when you meet a stranger who feels like a friend, and letting yourself take more than you should.

Hunter's been driving for what seems like hours. We've been on the highway and off again, along main streets and back roads, alternating one after the other. I know we were heading south earlier, but now? I have no idea where we are.

I guess that's the point.

The adrenaline from our escape has worn off. I'm completely exhausted, and yet too anxious to sleep. Hunter must be running on fumes, but he's awake and alert, his gaze focused on the road. Every minute or so he checks the rearview, constantly on the lookout to make sure we don't have a tail.

I have so many questions for him but don't dare ask them now. I wish he'd talk about *something*, though, because the silence is killing me.

Till now I'd been fiddling with the radio, playing deejay for this long, awkward road trip. But we've reached the point where we're outside any broadcast areas, and this old car doesn't have anything more than a cassette player and an AM/FM receiver.

It'd be nice to be able to distract myself with a game on my phone or something, but Hunter stashed it away in some alley by the club, worried that whoever is after me would be able to trace the signal to our whereabouts.

I sigh and sink back against the headrest. The brush scattered along the side of the road is nothing more than a blur in the darkness, illuminated by the headlights and then gone.

Every so often I'm tempted to turn and full-on admire Hunter here in the dark. There's something about the way the shadows cut across his face that makes him even more beautiful than he is in the light. Maybe it has something to do with the intense look in his eyes, the focus that he has on keeping me safe. I know it's his job, but having that intensity and protectiveness focused on me when I'm already attracted to him is a deadly combination. I could easily let myself get carried away and do something completely embarrassing like climb across the seat and attach my lips to his neck and see what his skin tastes like.

I tell myself it's just the adrenaline talking and that this one-sided attraction will die down once we reach our destination and I can get some space away from him. The whole idea of tonight was that I'd hook up and move on. I can't cut and run on Hunter, and I definitely don't want something more, so maybe this is for the best.

This unrelenting desire is the same feeling that got me in trouble with Carson, and I do *not* want to go down that road again.

"You doing all right?" Hunter finally asks, startling me.

"Yeah," I reply. "I don't want to *are we there yet* you, but… are we there yet?"

Hunter grins, which isn't the reaction I expected. "Bored?"

"The beginning of my evening was a little more exciting, yeah," I tease, hoping to open him up a bit so we can at least pass the time with some conversation.

"I wouldn't be very good at my job if I kept you in danger instead of getting you out of it, would I? The rest of our time together is going to be a real let-down if you're expecting more of what you got earlier tonight."

"Approximately how long are you expecting the rest of our time together to be, exactly?"

He shrugs. "Rest of the weekend, tops. You won't even miss any work."

"Wow." My eyes widen. I'm not exactly sure how long I expected this little escapade to last, but a day or two seems like a pretty generous timeline.

"You're surprised."

"Yeah, a little."

"We've located the threat, and removed you from the threat." He checks the rearview mirror, refocuses on the road before us. "Now all that's left is to neutralize the threat."

"That sounds ominous," I say, aiming for teasing but falling short.

"It doesn't have to be. You'd be surprised at what can convince people to change their minds about something," he replies with an easy smile. "It doesn't always require force."

"So...*you* don't neutralize the threat?" I ask.

"Sometimes," he replies, glancing at me out of the corner of his eye. "It depends on what the threat is. There are guys that work for me who have past ties to the group that Carson owes money to. Their experience is more beneficial in shutting them down. My experience is more beneficial to you here, getting you out of town and protecting you in case one of them miraculously finds us."

"What exactly are the chances of a miracle here?" I ask.

"Slim to none."

"Okay, good to know." Trusting in a complete stranger isn't easy, but he hasn't given me any reason to think he'd lie about potential danger. "It's not that I didn't believe you when you said I was in good hands—"

"Alexa's in good hands," he corrects.

"Oh...kay," I say slowly, not sure where this is going.

"I told you Alexa is in good hands, and she is." Hunter tears his eyes away from the road, pinning me with a look that's so intense it makes my breath catch. "You're in the *best* hands."

I don't want to read into things that aren't there. I mean,

protecting me is literally Hunter's job, and the flirting at the club must have been part of a ruse to lure me in without scaring me. But there's such *intent* behind his words. He's looking at me like this *means* something, and I could've sworn he'd wanted to kiss me back in that alley…and no. *No*, I can't let myself go there.

"So," I say, drawing the word out as I trace the hem of my dress, trying to turn the conversation in a different direction before I do something completely embarrassing like crawl onto his lap and kiss him. "No high-speed car chases is what you're saying."

Hunter shakes his head. "No chases of any kind if I do my job right. And I *always* do my job right."

"Good to know." If my voice shakes a little, Hunter doesn't seem to notice.

"So you can relax. The scary part is over, no one's going to hurt you."

"I don't know. The scary part wasn't as scary as it could've been," I tell him, before I can think better of it. "You have a very calming way about you, even in circumstances that don't exactly warrant calm."

I glance in Hunter's direction and catch his smile before it disappears.

"Is this the way you always operate? On the fly like this? You said earlier that you didn't plan on introducing yourself to me the way you did." A flurry of other questions fly into my mind even before he answers the ones I've just asked. "How did you find me? Would it creep me out?"

"Not as much as the way the other guys found you."

My body shudders involuntarily. That this could've been going on for god knows how long without me knowing…an icy cold shiver works its way across my spine at the mere thought of being watched.

Knowing what I know now, I realize that it's going to take

a long time for my life to go back to the way it was, assuming it ever does. Walking around oblivious, assuming I had my privacy...those days are over. But that's a train of thought I can chase later, when I'm back at home in my bed and my life looks a little more like I remember it.

"Then don't tell me," I say. "I don't want to know."

Hunter tears his eyes from the road, watching me carefully. "Are you sure?"

"I'm sure," I tell Hunter. "Do my parents know about this?"

Hunter shakes his head. "No. I thought it was best to limit the circle of people who knew what was happening, since we're expecting to be able to take care of it pretty quickly. Did you want them to?"

"No!" I say quickly, then take a deep breath to calm the panic. "No. They weren't Carson's biggest fans. They warned me of him, but I didn't listen. I thought I knew him better than they did." I let out a bitter laugh. "Turns out I was wrong."

"I understand that feeling."

"It's a real bitch, isn't it?"

With a laugh, Hunter turns and looks at me. "It definitely is."

"You know, this is probably an awkward time to bring this up, but I can't pay you for any of this," I explain. "I mean, I don't know what the hourly rate for private security is, but I do know that I don't have it."

"It's already taken care of."

I glance over at him with a raised brow. "What does that mean?"

"It means that *you* don't have to pay me."

"And your boss is okay with that?"

He smiles. "I *am* the boss."

Oh, well...that was sexier than it should have been. I want

to push him on it, but I decide not to, given that he's put his life on the line for mine tonight. Asking about how he's getting compensated seems rude.

"I don't really understand why these guys would come after me," I admit. "Carson and I broke up a year and a half ago. It did *not* end well. That someone would try to use me as leverage over him…I don't get it. He had to have said something that made them believe it, since I wouldn't be here otherwise, but…"

"There wasn't a lot of time for him to get into the whole story," Hunter says, drumming his fingertips across the steering wheel. "He didn't come to me until it was almost too late. But I think that when someone's as far gone as he is, they grab on to the last good thing they had and romanticize it, thinking that as long as they have that, they'll keep a piece of the person they used to be. Maybe that's what Carson is doing with you."

My stomach flips uneasily considering that possibility. It makes me feel unfathomably sad and angry all at once.

"He didn't want help, and I couldn't give him what he wanted. I *wouldn't* give him what he wanted, because it was too much."

Hunter nods sympathetically. "When someone's drowning, you don't have to let them take you down too."

The pain in his voice is unmistakable. "It sounds like you have some experience with this yourself."

"Generally, yes," he admits. "Specifically with Carson."

That shocks the hell out of me, but the more I think about it, the more this whole situation makes sense. It's a favor, not a job.

"He's a friend?"

Hunter lets out a sharp, bitter laugh. "No. More like…a responsibility."

I'm not sure what to make of it, and I don't want to pry, but I desperately want to know more.

We're quiet for a mile or two, then Hunter turns to me. "You aren't going to ask?"

"I want to know, but only if you want to tell me. If your experience with him is anything like mine, I imagine it's not an easy story to tell."

"He was a friend of my brother's," Hunter says after a long pause. "Bobby liked to party, and Carson was new in town, looking for some friends. Bobby was always happy to get people involved in his lifestyle, and...it, uh..." Hunter anxiously rubs the back of his neck. "It didn't end well for Bobby. I was hoping I could keep Carson from meeting the same fate."

After my own experience with Carson even before he hit rock bottom, I have nothing but admiration for someone who stuck around and tried pulling him out of the depths of his addiction.

It's mostly a losing battle, but every day you have to wake up ready to fight.

"You're a good person," I tell him.

I don't know much about Hunter, but I do know that.

"You know, you're taking this pretty well."

It's taken a good fifteen minutes for the heaviness between us to dissipate, but I'm glad to move on to a *somewhat* lighter topic. "It's a little too surreal to digest at the moment," I admit. "You probably won't think I'm dealing so well when the fear insomnia kicks in tonight."

Hunter reaches out, places his warm hand on the sleeve of his jacket, which I'm still wearing. "You're safe with me, you know that, right?"

His eyes are incredibly earnest, even in the dark shadows of this beat-up old car. And the truth is, I do know that. Trust isn't something that's easily earned with me, but based on what he's done for me this strange night, in these strange circumstances? Hunter definitely has mine.

"I do know that."

He gives a decisive nod at my confirmation. "It's okay if you need to freak out. You don't have to pretend like you're dealing if you're not. I can listen, lend you a shoulder to cry on. Anything."

"It's not that I don't appreciate the offer, because I do," I tell him. "But freaking out isn't going to change the fact that tonight definitely didn't go the way I hoped it would. And it won't stop whoever's shooting at me from shooting at me. It'll just give you a distraction that you clearly don't need, and it's not going to make me feel better anyway.

"So, don't think that because I'm not freaking out that I'm not terrified. I am. I…*was.* But you asked me to trust you and proved that I could, so…that's what I'm doing. Besides," I continue, trying to break up my awkward ramble, "I figured after throwing your body on mine to keep me from getting shot that crying on your shoulder wasn't the best way to repay you."

Hunter full-on smiles, more gorgeous than he has any right being at a time like this. "The offer stands whether you take it up or not," he explains. "For as long as we're together, and after, if you need."

"Thank you."

I don't have much time to dwell on said offer, because Hunter takes a right onto a dimly lit street, and all of a sudden we're back in some kind of civilization. It's not much of a town from what little I'm able to make out, but it's something. The neon sign for a diner lights up the corner at the end of a long row of what looks like a lot of empty store-

31

fronts. Another right takes us down a street littered with a few houses here and there, long stretches of road in between them.

A left turn and a short ride down a narrow, bumpy gravel road later, Hunter brings the car to a stop in front of a cabin that looks like it has dubious structural integrity.

"Stay here for a sec," Hunter says, taking the keys and locking me in behind him.

I have absolutely no desire to venture out of this car until he gives me the okay, so I do what he tells me to.

Hunter walks along the perimeter of the place. It's so tiny that he's barely out of sight for more than a few seconds. He returns to the car, pops the trunk, and rummages around back there for a while. The car creaks as Hunter lowers the trunk lid, and then he opens my door.

"C'mon," he says with a gentle smile, holding out his hand.

He pulls me up, and I shuffle my feet a little, thankful to have some good blood flow after being stuck in the car for god knows how long. He makes his way to the front door, a huge duffel slung over his broad shoulder, dragging a cooler in tow.

He jiggles a few keys in a few locks, and when the door opens with a high-pitched squeal, he enters a code on the touch pad on the wall.

"What is this place?" I ask, stepping over the threshold.

"It's a *safe* place," he replies, dropping the bag by the floor and taking the cooler over to the kitchen, which is on the far side of the main living area—what appears to be the majority of this cabin. "And it's what we're calling home for the fore-seeable future."

Even though it's a little musty, it's a whole hell of a lot nicer on the inside than you'd guess by looking at the outside. Don't judge a book by its cover and all that.

The cabin resembles a studio apartment, with a fairly modern-looking kitchen on the far side of the room. There's a little bathroom off to the right. The walls are painted in a homey yellow, and there are pictures—photos of people and landscapes—hanging here and there.

There are worse places to stay when you're running for your life.

Only problem is, there's just one bed.

CHAPTER
Four

I keep an eye on Hayley as I unload the contents of the cooler into the fridge. She stands in the middle of the great room, hands twisted together, taking in her surroundings.

"What do you think of the place?" I ask, dropping a bag of apples into the crisper.

"It's nicer than I expected," Hayley replies. Her eyes immediately widen.

She's so refreshingly honest that I can't help but smile. "I'm glad you think so. I want you to be comfortable here, so make yourself at home."

She blushes a pretty pink. "I didn't mean to insult the place," she explains quickly. "It's just that looking at it from the outside, I wasn't expecting it to be so nice on the inside." She tugs a strand of hair behind her ear, presses her lips together, and looks down at the ground. "I didn't make it any better, did I?"

"It's fine," I tell her, putting a carton of orange juice on the top shelf.

"We seem pretty off the grid. I can't imagine anyone tracking me down here, so if your goal was to make me feel safe, then you succeeded. That it's a nice place is just a bonus."

"It's not much to look at right now," I tell her. "It has a lot of sentimental value, though. I can't get down here as much as I'd like, so I'm only able to work on it every once in a while. I've done what I could on the inside. Now I've got to work on the outside."

Hayley's eyes brighten with surprise. "This is yours?"

I nod slowly, totally amused. "Did you think we were at a random cabin in the woods, or…"

"No," she replies quickly, followed by a shrug. "I don't know? I thought this was a bodyguard network safe house or something."

I laugh. "No. We do have a couple of safe houses we can use, but this was a little too last-minute to count on that. I had to do some quick thinking with you."

"Ah, I bet you say that to all the girls you bring here," she teases.

"You're the only one I've ever brought here." The admission slips out unexpectedly and hangs heavily in the air.

We stare at each other a beat too long, then she breaks the silence with an amused huff. "You have Fort Knox-level security at this cabin in the woods you never bring people to?" She hitches her thumb over her shoulder, in the direction of the security system's keypad on the wall by the front door.

I close the fridge and cross my arms over my chest. "You don't know much about Fort Knox, do you?"

Hayley grins.

I walk over to the door and grab the black duffel I carried in with us, then drop it on the bed.

"What's in there?" Hayley asks.

"One of my female agents guessed at your sizes and packed some things for you to wear."

She slides her thumbs along the straps of her dress. "You don't like what I'm wearing?"

She's teasing me, but I can't help myself; my gaze travels across her body. The dress teases me with the fullness of her breasts, makes me want to hike up the skirt and lick along her curves. Liking it is a total understatement, and it's probably for the best if she changes out of it immediately.

"I like it very much," I tell her, my voice a little choked.

She bites her bottom lip and looks down at the ground as her fingers play with the fabric. "Look, Hunter…we met in a pretty unconventional way, and I don't want you to feel bad about what you had to do in order to keep me safe. I really do appreciate it," she says as she takes a step back. "What happened at the club—me hitting on you, you pretending to hit on me—and after, in the alley, I just…I wanted to let you know that there are no hard feelings since none of that was *real*."

It's unconscionable to let her go on thinking I didn't mean what I did, what I said, but her life is in my hands. It's better to not complicate things.

"It was real for *me*, is what I meant. I wasn't…" She shakes her head, seeming a little frustrated. "I'm not expecting anything from you, is all. Not that I think that you think I was, but just in case. I'm going to stop talking now."

She looks at me with hopeful eyes, and it takes everything

I have in me to stick with my plan of not making this complicated. It would help me out greatly if she covered up a little.

"Here," I tell her, unzipping the duffel. "You must be tired."

"I'm kind of tired," she admits a little too brightly. "But I'm not sure I'm going to be able to sleep."

"You need to try." It's been a long night, and the crash is going to hit her sooner than later. "There's something in there for you to sleep in."

Hayley digs through the clothes, placing them in a neat stack on the bed. "Well, your agent did a great job at picking out stuff I would like," she says, placing her hands on her hips. "But she did an awful job at putting pajamas in there."

"Really?"

She nods. "Really."

I take a deep breath, then walk over to my chest of drawers and pull out a T-shirt. Seeing her in one of my shirts isn't going to help this situation at all. I'm tempted just to ask her to sleep in the damn dress. "Here," I say, handing it over. "You can wear this. The bathroom's over there."

She snags a small toiletry kit from the duffel, takes the T-shirt and walks into the bathroom, closing the door behind her.

With Hayley occupied in the bathroom, I change into an old pair of sweatpants I had in my bottom drawer, then toss some sheets on the floor next to the door for me to sleep on. With nothing left to do, and impatient for Hayley to come out, I sit on the edge of the bed and text Davis to see if there's any news.

He replies almost immediately. We're making headway quicker than I thought we would.

I'm so wrapped up in my reply that I don't hear Hayley coming out of the bathroom. Instead, I feel her eyes on me from all the way across the room.

I look up and see her staring, mouth slightly open. I'd be amused at her reaction to seeing me shirtless if I wasn't so caught up in the way she's swimming in my T-shirt. The gray cotton cuts off on her thigh, just this side of indecent.

"Shirt okay?" I ask, voice raspy as she tosses her dress over my jacket on the back of the chair by the door.

"Yes, thank you," she replies, seeming unsure of herself.

"I'm gonna sleep on the floor. You can take the bed."

"Oh. Okay."

She seems a little disappointed, which makes my gut twist in a way I'd rather not think about with her standing in front of me looking the way she does.

"Oh my god," she says, rushing over. "You're bleeding!"

I look down at the gash on my bicep and give a little shrug. "It's not bleeding anymore."

Hayley's eyes widen, and she places her palm on her chest. "You got *shot*?" She gently slides her fingertips along the swollen flesh around the wound, her touch soothing the sting that's persisted the past few hours.

"I got *grazed*," I insist. "I've been shot before, and this is nothing." Ruined my favorite shirt, but that's about it. I place my hand over hers, giving it a gentle pat. "Don't worry about it, it's part of the job."

"It doesn't look like nothing to me," Hayley argues. "And it shouldn't be part of the job!" She examines it closely with a cute look that quickly kills my annoyance with her blowing this out of proportion. "Are you just going to leave it open like that?"

"I cleaned it up with the first-aid kit while you were in the bathroom." This is mostly true. I did wipe around it with an alcohol pad.

"Shouldn't you at least put a bandage on it so it doesn't get infected?"

I playfully roll my eyes. It's nothing, really, but it's nice to have someone worry. To have someone take care of me. It's been a long time since I've had someone in my life who did either.

"Where's the first-aid kit?" she asks.

I make a play of reluctantly nodding toward the kitchen counter. She walks over, plucks out some sterile gauze and medical tape, then plants herself on the bed, next to me. The shirt she's wearing rides up dangerously high, so I studiously examine the floor in an attempt to remove temptation.

"You should've said something." She rips open a packet of gauze.

"There were more important things going on. If it's a choice between tending to a flesh wound and keeping you safe, I'm keeping you safe."

"Impossible man," she grumbles, pressing the gauze against the wound and reaching for the tape.

I let out a short laugh. She's cute when she's exasperated. "It really is nothing," I say softly.

"Maybe to you." She secures the tape, her fingers warm and reassuring against my skin, leaving a pleasant tingling in their wake. "But this happened because of me, so bandaging it makes me feel better. It's the least I can do."

"It didn't happen because of you. But if it makes *you* feel better," I reply with an easy smile. Teasing her is fun, and I like the way she bites her lip to hide her smile when I do it.

We stare at each other a little longer than necessary, then Hayley quickly closes the first-aid kit and bolts upright.

In her attempt to make a quick escape, she trips on my foot, and I reach out, placing my hands on her hips to steady her.

"Be careful. Otherwise I'll have to bandage *you* up." I

mean it as a joke, but her skin is soft and I'm absentmindedly rubbing small circles where I hold her. We get stuck in this…moment.

Which we both realize at the same time, because I let go of her right as she steps out of my reach.

"Thank you," I say as she nearly falls over herself again in her rush to get back to the kitchen.

I stand and grab a pillow, then toss it down on my makeshift bed.

"Want me to leave the light on?"

She hesitates, nervously twisting her fingers together.

"No," she finally replies. "But thank you for asking."

I wait as she tucks herself in, then flip off the light, lie down and get settled.

"Goodnight, Hayley."

She whispers, "Goodnight."

CHAPTER
Five

I wake to bright rays of sunshine slamming me directly in the face. I groan and burrow my head into my pillow, catching the smell of fresh-brewed coffee as I move. That perks me up.

I slide my legs over the edge of the bed, taking a second to get my bearings. The sheets and pillows that were on the floor last night are gone, the open duffel bag sitting in their place.

"Good morning," Hunter says, leaning against the kitchen counter, holding a mug in his hands. "How'd you sleep?"

"I passed out as soon as my head hit the pillow."

"I know," he says with a wry smile, bringing the mug to his lips. "You were sawing logs all night."

"What?"

He lets out a totally exaggerated, obnoxious snore.

"I was not! I don't snore!"

"If you say so," Hunter replies, smiling.

I grab a pillow off the bed and toss it across the room at him, coming up way, way short.

"Coffee? Might help your aim."

I need caffeination. I can't even be mad. "Yes, I'd like all of the coffee please."

Hunter laughs as he plucks a cup from one of the shelves next to the sink. He fills it, then holds it out to me. "Sugar's over there, and if you want cream, all I have is that non-dairy powdered stuff."

I take the cup from him gratefully, then spoon a little sugar in there. "Thank you."

"I'm making breakfast. Are bacon and eggs okay? I wasn't sure if you were a vegetarian or…"

"No," I reply quickly. "I pretty much consider bacon a food group." Hunter laughs. "But you don't have to make me breakfast, I can do it myself."

"Absolutely not," he replies, reaching into the fridge and pulling out a carton of eggs and a thick slab of bacon. "You're a guest."

I can't help but laugh. "You make it sound like I'm here voluntarily."

"Is my company *that* bad?" he teases.

"If you feel responsible for this thing with Carson because you feel responsible for him, please don't. I'd be in this mess regardless, and without you I wouldn't have a way to get out of it. If anyone should be making breakfast, I should be making it for you. Besides, I did keep you up all night. And not in the fun way."

Hunter chokes a little on his coffee, then shakes his head. "No. No way. I'm cooking."

I'm not going to argue with him. "Okay, but I'll do the cleanup."

He ponders that for a moment. "You can *help* with the cleanup."

"Deal," I reply with a smile. "Is it okay if I ask what's going to happen to him? You get him out of this mess, and then what? He gets involved with shady people to get money for a high *again*, they come after me to collect on his debt *again*?"

With a stony look in his eyes, Hunter says, "No one is ever going to come after you again, okay? Once this is over for you, it's over for you, Hayley. You won't have to live in fear when you leave your house every day."

He's so vehement about it that it makes my heart skip. "You can't guarantee that, Hunter. And I'm not asking you to."

"Hayley—"

"I've known Carson for years," he explains, reaching out and taking my hand. "When he reached out to me this time, he looked…I've never seen him like this. He wants help, and I'm going to make sure he gets it. And I'm going to make sure that you don't have to worry about this anymore."

Seems like Hunter knows as well as I do that wanting help and accepting it are not the same thing, and that a relapse is more likely than not. But he desperately wants to believe in this, and I'm not going to be the one who takes that hope away from him. Selfishly, I want to believe, too.

"Don't let him take you down with him, okay?" I say, squeezing his fingers. I know how easy it is to get sucked into someone else's toxicity. "Don't let his life choices affect yours."

The corner of Hunter's mouth quirks up into an almost-smile. "Carson and I rarely have direct contact," he admits.

"One of my guys is a former drug counselor, and he acts as an intermediary. After my brother's overdose…" Hunter looks down, eyes locked on the floor. "It's too hard."

"With someone who's done as much damage as Carson has, it's commendable that you're able to be involved at all. Even through a third party," I tell him. And then inevitable tears prick at my eyes and make it difficult to swallow. "And thank you for making sure he doesn't touch my life more than he already has."

"In the interest of full disclosure," he says, letting his fingers fall from mine. "I've been doing that for a while now."

Puzzled, I ask, "What?"

"I know you have a restraining order against him," Hunter admits. "I…kind of made sure he didn't violate it, that he kept his distance from you. It wasn't easy at first, but I got him a job and he managed to get somewhat straight for a while, and then all hell broke loose."

"Wow," I say, stunned. Guess Carson adhering to the terms wasn't so miraculous after all.

"I didn't just do it for you." Hunter cringes as the words leave his mouth. He backs up a little, then leans against the countertop, folding his arms across his broad chest. "I mean, I didn't know you, I just knew your name. And I didn't want Carson harassing you, but mostly I didn't want him winding up in jail. I thought that if he got into the system that all hope for him would be gone, but now?" He scrubs his face with his hands. "Maybe that would've been the best thing for him. Maybe it *is*."

"You're just not ready to give up yet."

He nods, and I reach out and put my hand on his arm.

"I hope he doesn't disappoint you."

I gave up on Carson for my own good after six months. That Hunter is still here however many years and however many fuckups later speaks volumes about the kind of person he is. And even though the circumstances under which we met are awful, I can't help but feel like meeting him was a stroke of luck for me.

"Me too," Hunter replies.

"Now," I say, wanting to lighten things up a bit, "if I remember correctly, you said something about breakfast. Bacon, specifically."

With a grin, Hunter ignites a burner and puts a pan on top. "Coming right up." He nods toward the table. "Have a seat."

I take my coffee cup and settle down into a seat. "Have you heard from whoever is with Alexa? Is she okay?"

Hunter reaches into his pocket and pulls out his phone, tapping out a quick message to someone before he walks over and hands it to me. "When it rings it'll be for you."

Two seconds later, it does. I nearly drop the phone in my hurry to answer it.

"Hello?"

"Oh my god. Are you okay?" It's never felt so good to hear Alexa's voice.

"I'm okay. Are *you* okay?"

"If I ever see Carson again, I'm gonna kick him in the dick. Twice," she says breathlessly.

"I won't stop you."

"Where are you?"

I stand and walk over by the bed, just to give myself a little privacy. "In the middle of nowhere." I catch Hunter glancing over his shoulder. "Where are you?"

"In my apartment with a wall of muscle who's fun to flirt with. He's hot. Is your guy hot?"

I can't help but laugh. That's Alexa, always asking the important questions. I look over at Hunter, his back turned as he tends to our breakfast. "Yeah."

"Well," she sighs, "if there's an upside to nearly getting

45

killed at a club before you found someone to take home for the night, maybe this is it."

"I'm glad you're enjoying yourself," I tease.

"Seriously though," Alexa says, her voice somber. "I'm glad you're okay. That scared the shit out of me."

"Me too." I take a deep breath, trying really hard not to think about it any more than I have to.

"Hey, my guy wants to talk to your guy."

"He's making breakfast," I tell her.

She makes a delighted little squee. "Maybe he's a keeper after all."

"Stop it. I'll see you soon."

"Love you," she says.

"Love you."

Hunter flips an egg that sizzles in the pan, then I tap him on the shoulder and hand him the phone.

My stomach growls as he's talking. I'm so hungry, and the cabin smells amazing. Maybe Alexa was right; there are definitely worse things that could happen the morning after being shot at than having a hot bodyguard cook you breakfast. I get a little lost in the way Hunter's back muscles move beneath his tight T-shirt as he reaches into a cabinet and pulls down a couple plates.

"Hey," he says with a smirk as he catches me staring. "Alexa asked me to pass along a message."

That gets my attention away from his body. "Oh yeah? What is it?"

"She said she hopes you found what you were looking for last night."

Oh god.

After the breakfast dishes are washed and dried, I'm standing in the middle of the cabin in an outfit I fished out of the duffel bag, looking at the pictures that decorate the walls.

The first one I zoom in on is a photo of what looks like a young Hunter with a much older man. "Is this your grandfather?"

Hunter nods from where he sits at the kitchen table. "Yes. This was his cabin."

"And now it's yours."

"He left it to me when he died. It was just a place he liked to go to get away from life and spend some time fishing," he says with a fond smile. "I try to keep up the tradition."

"You come down here a lot?"

"I do," he says. "Whenever I get a chance, usually once a month. It's tough to schedule time away with my job, because things come up last minute."

"I bet they do." I wonder what he was up to yesterday before he rushed off to the club to make sure I was safe, how many times his plans have been interrupted so he can do the same thing for some other person. "How did you even get into the business, if you don't mind me asking?"

"I started working personal security when I got out of college. Actors, musicians, you name it. I've always had what my mom refers to as an 'innate need to protect people,'" he says, using air quotes.

"I definitely see that," I tell him. From what I've learned about him in what little bit of time I've spent with him, he seems like the type who wants to look out for any and everyone he can. It's an admirable and charming trait, but I can see how it would get in the way of having a normal kind of life.

"After a year or so, I really wanted to get into lower-profile stuff, so I started working with an ex-Special Forces guy who took a liking to me, and when he retired, I bought him out."

"And now you're working on thrilling jobs like making me amazing bacon and eggs."

"Yes, it's definitely one of my more exciting assignments," he replies with a wink.

"I think you mean 'egg-citing.'"

Hunter lets out a full-bodied laugh. His smile and dimple are so gorgeous, as is the amused sparkle in his eye when he looks at me. The thrill that I get at making him laugh at my dad joke is lame, but I can't help it.

There are a few more pictures of Hunter and his grandfather, and some of who I'm guessing is his grandmother, too. Then I come across one that's set apart from the rest, in a gold frame on the nightstand.

It's a young boy, maybe fifteen or sixteen. He has hair like Hunter's, but his chin is a little longer, his nose a little bigger. There's a playful charm in the way he smiles proudly as he holds up a huge fish in front of a shimmering lake. I know who it is without asking, but I ask anyway.

"Is this your brother?"

Hunter pauses. "Bobby, yeah," he answers, his voice rough.

"Was this his first big catch?"

"It was his first catch. Period." I can actually see Hunter's love for his brother written all over his face when he says, "He wasn't big on the outdoors, but Grandpa and I tried." There's a sadness in his eyes that quickly takes over, one that I've seen in myself when I was in the depths of my turbulent relationship with Carson.

"Is this lake nearby?" I ask, grasping at anything I can to change the subject.

"It's right outside." Hunter points to the window next to me, obscured by curtains.

"Is it okay for me to open these?"

Hunter stands, walks over, and gently pulls back the

curtain. Not that I want to be casual with my safety, but… "Is there a high likelihood of someone lurking outside?"

"I just wanted to check first."

"Innate need to protect people?" I tease.

"Something like that," he replies with a grin.

I rest my hands on the window ledge—it's higher than normal, about chest level—and raise myself up to get a good look. I couldn't see it last night in the dark, but this property is gorgeous. There's a ring of trees surrounding the lake, and a small pier jutting out into the water, a boat tied to one of the posts. The morning sunshine shimmers against the surface of the water, and the whole scene looks a lot like a spread in a travel magazine. Idyllic.

"You own this?" I ask incredulously. "The lake and everything?"

"The lake and everything."

"Everything the light touches is your kingdom." I say in a comically low voice that's actually a terrible impression of the original.

Hunter doesn't even try to hide his confusion. "What?"

I shake my head, feeling a little silly. "Never mind. It's from a movie. I'm jealous you own an actual lake. I bet that was fun to swim in when you were a kid."

With a nostalgic glint in his eye, he says, "It was."

"I've never done it, but I've always wanted to, ever since I was a kid."

Hunter gives me this look, kind of like I've grown a second head.

"What? Not all dreams are big ones."

He laughs.

"I watched a lot of *Dirty Dancing* when I was a kid."

His brows knit together adorably. "I don't follow."

"Have you ever seen it?"

"A long time ago, yeah," he admits.

"So, when Johnny and Baby were practicing for their big dance at the Sheldrake, they had to do a lift. They get in a lake to practice so that the water will break Baby's fall." I'm almost embarrassingly excited about this explanation, but it's too late to reel it in now. "Anyway, they're in the water. Johnny's shirtless, and Baby has on this see-through white tank top, and the two of them are laughing and having fun together for pretty much the first time in the whole movie, and there was all this sexual tension." I let out a dreamy sigh. "That was peak romance for me when I was younger."

Hunter just smiles at me like I'm the most adorable thing he's ever seen. It's a good look on him, but I kind of hate it. There are a lot of things I'd like Hunter to think about me, but that I'm adorable is certainly not high on that list.

"I don't suppose swimming is on the itinerary this weekend?"

For a split second, this feels like a regular conversation under regular circumstances. Last night at the club, when people were *shooting at me* feels like days ago. Another *lifetime* ago.

"Sorry," he says. It actually sounds like he means it. "Can't take the risk."

"I thought you were confident in your abilities? We're out in the middle of nowhere!" I'm trying for a teasing kind of persuasion, but Hunter must've heard every excuse in the book for people wanting to do things they shouldn't, because he isn't swayed.

"I'm confident, not careless. We can do anything you want, as long as it's within these four walls."

"Anything I want?"

He nods slowly, looking a little caught.

I can definitely work with that. "Okay."

Turns out I can't work with that.

Normally I'd be ecstatic at the prospect of a blank check for fun, but I'm having difficulty imagining what we could possibly get up to in this confined little cabin in the middle of nowhere since my first choice—lots of what I'm sure would be amazing, commitment-free sex—is solidly off the table. Much as it pains me, Hunter isn't interested.

There isn't even a board game in the place. Hunter digs out a puzzle with a giant hole in the corner of the box from a dark corner in his closet. We manage to get most of the edge put together before we realize that there are pieces missing, because *of course* there are.

I find a deck of cards in the junk drawer in the kitchen, but a few cards are missing from that deck, too. Hunter tells me he thinks his grandfather pitched them, to make sure he and his brother didn't stay inside all day when there was so much nature around them.

For someone who got dragged out of her apartment because she was spending too much time in it, I'm surprisingly going stir-crazy. Turns out having Netflix on hand makes time go by a lot faster when you're bored, and it turns out that wanting what you can't have makes you want it even more. I'm learning that lesson double time here, both with Hunter and the fact that I'd give pretty much anything to be able to go outside right now, even if I have to stay in this podunk town.

Hunter's handling things better than I am. He's sitting at the small table in the kitchen, leaning back in the chair that creaks every time he moves, completely involved in whatever he's looking at on his phone. Occasionally his brow furrows, but he doesn't give anything else away. From the looks of it, he'd be perfectly happy to hang out here for all eternity.

He's probably used to taking these little excursions to protect other clients, and at least he's engrossed in his work.

There's a relatively steady stream of calls coming in, and all I know from what few words I'm able to make out from Hunter's hushed tone is that things are going well and they're close to "closing the deal" with some guy named Damien.

My understanding is that Damien is the reason why I'm stuck in this godforsaken cabin with nothing to do, forced in the orbit of a gorgeous man I can't touch. So, the sooner whatever the "deal" is gets closed, the better off I'll be.

I'm getting restless, pacing the room for lack of anything better to do, wanting to lace up my sneakers and run for the first time in forever, if only because I know that I can't do that. There's a nervous energy bubbling up inside me, making me feel like I'm going to come out of my skin.

"Restless?" Hunter asks from his spot at the table, where he looks perfectly content. Jerk.

I let out a humorless huff of a laugh. "What gave it away? The pacing or the way I'm clenching and unclenching my fists?"

My sarcasm doesn't even make him flinch. "If you need an outlet, I could teach you some self-defense," he says, setting his phone face down on the table. I'd swear it almost looks like he regrets it the second the words come out of his mouth, but he doesn't take them back.

This isn't exactly the offer I was hoping for, but an outlet for all this pent-up energy would be nice.

"After last night, it wouldn't hurt for you to be able to protect yourself."

"There's a self-defense technique that can make you bulletproof?" I tease, feeling lighter at the prospect of getting to do *something* soon.

He shakes his head, smiling as he tilts his head down. "No," he sighs. "But short of being bulletproof, you should at the very least know the basics. I teach self-defense classes for women. Consider this one on the house."

I hate to admit it, but he has a point. The likelihood of a drug dealer's minions coming after me for money that my ex owes them by raining down a hail of gunfire in a club I'm at seems relatively small. Having Hunter in such close proximity, though, with sweating and touching and all *that* torture? Seems like a terrible idea, but I never again want to be completely powerless in a situation like I was in last night.

"Sound good?" Hunter asks.

It's bad. It's a really, really bad idea for so many reasons, but I'm going to do it anyway.

"Self-defense? Sounds great."

CHAPTER
Six

The second I press my chest against her back to show her the proper stance to defend against an attack, I realize just how bad this idea was on my part. I had an inkling when I offered and almost took it back, but I'm a certified self-defense instructor. I teach women all the time. I've never been so insanely attracted to any of them, granted. I thought I could detach into teacher mode and turn everything off.

I can't.

What was I thinking? I have a hard enough time keeping myself in check with Hayley even without physical contact, and here she is letting me touch her. Even though, theoretically, it's a great idea—she *needs* to learn how to throw a punch or take down a would-be assailant—I'm the last person who should be teaching her this.

She should be taught by someone who isn't thinking about how warm and soft her skin is. Even after all night in a bar followed by a road trip in an old beat-up car, I still catch a whiff of her fruity shampoo when she turns her head. Her perfume still lingers on her skin; there's a hint of it in the air when I show her how to hold her fist for a punch. Her skin is soft beneath my fingers.

I shake my head, hoping it'll clear all the thoughts I definitely shouldn't be having right now. I need to focus on her safety, not on *her*.

"This is just basic self-defense," I tell her, desperate to get myself in the right frame of mind. "It's not enough to take on anyone with a weapon, but I'll teach you a basic disarming technique in case someone gets close enough to you with a knife or a gun. Even if they don't have a weapon at all, you'll be able to stun them for long enough to get away."

"I know it's best to be prepared, but I really hope I don't ever have to use any of this."

"I hope you don't either." I can't stand the thought of someone trying to hurt her, making her fear for her life the way she did in the club last night. I could go a lifetime without seeing that panic on her face again. I want her to be able to take control and not be at the mercy of a stranger who wants to do her harm, on the off chance that there's a next time. "If a man puts his hands on you and you don't want them there, I'm going to show you how to make sure you can get them off and keep yourself safe."

It'll be difficult to do here without any gloves, mats, or props that I usually use, but I can teach her the basics without full force.

She nods, taking the defensive stance I just taught her. It

isn't perfect, but 30 minutes into the lesson I wouldn't expect perfection.

We practice until she has relatively good form with a straight punch, a groin kick, and a knee kick. Hayley is a quick study, and she's stronger than I anticipated.

"Do you work out?" I ask, wanting to get a feel for other ways I could teach her to use her natural strength.

Hayley hesitates, sliding her plump bottom lip through her teeth and nearly making me groan. I'd done such a great job of slipping into the teacher headspace, and now all I want to do is kiss her and find out what she tastes like.

"Not as much as I did before I moved to D.C.," she explains, pulling me out of the fantasy brewing in my mind. "In college I was on the volleyball team, and I'm competitive as hell. Staying in the gym gave me an edge, so I was there pretty much all the time."

That makes me smile. It explains why her punch is so strong, and why there's so much force behind her kicks. Strong as she is, though, the next part might be more of a challenge for her.

"Someone could try and grab you by caging you in with his arms," I explain. "They could put their arms around you from the front, which is rare, or sneak up on you from behind."

Hayley narrows her eyes, like she's thinking about the problem and trying to figure out the right way to respond to that threat based on what I've just taught her. I'm glad she's taking this so seriously.

"If he comes at me from the front, then I knee him in the groin," she replies proudly. "From behind, I...punch his forearms?" She demonstrates by curling her right hand in a fist, mimicking hitting her forearm by moving her hand up and down.

It's a good guess, but an incorrect one.

"For anyone who's bigger than you are, it'll be difficult for you to get away. Even with the groin kicks and punches we just rehearsed. In any situation where someone puts their arms around you and tries to overpower you, you have to be as difficult to control as possible."

I move up right behind her, pressing my chest against her back. She tenses and turns her head in my direction. "I'm not going to hurt you," I reassure her softly. I don't want her to think that this is real or that she needs to come at me full force.

She nods, giving me a soft smile that makes me want to kiss her. Again. I have to refocus, because I can't kiss her. Especially not now, when she's on the verge of learning a skill that's important. One that could save her life if she's ever in a situation like the one she was in last night.

"I know you won't."

I take a deep breath and clear my head, getting myself under control. "I can't think of a better analogy to use, but if you ever get into a situation like this, where some attacker gets their arms around you to try and control you, the best thing you can do is think of yourself like a wild animal," I tell her. I place my hand on her bicep, mimicking the motion she should use to push against my arms. "They'll do anything to escape when they think their lives are in danger. You need to squirm and wiggle as much as you can. Don't focus on any precision moves of hitting a particular area. Just crouch down, lower your center of gravity, and flail. Elbow, kick, whatever…but make it as hard as you can for them to hold on to you."

She shivers a little in my arms, probably imagining a scenario I hope like hell she's never in.

"Want to give it a try?" I ask.

She steps out of my embrace and raises her brows. "To be

clear, you don't want me to actually elbow you or knee you in the balls, right?"

I laugh. "Yeah, please don't do that. Just focus on trying to get away for now, steering clear of my balls."

I wouldn't blame her if she did want to knee me in the balls after I flirted with her in the club last night, then let her believe it was an act.

"Okay," she replies tentatively, which doesn't give me much confidence, but there's nothing I can do about that now.

"Ready?" I ask.

CHAPTER
Seven

I'm not ready.

Not ready for Hunter standing so close to me. Not ready for the way his breath sweeps across the back of my neck, making me shiver. Not ready for the way his ridiculously broad chest molds against my back.

Definitely not ready to feel his six-pack through the thin cotton of the T-shirt I'm wearing. Hunter's wearing a shirt, too. Those muscles are making themselves known through *two* layers of cotton. Just how built *is* this guy?

I don't answer, and Hunter takes that as his cue to go right ahead and slide his arms around me, moving slowly like he has during the first run of all the other moves he's taught me. Guess he figures I'm not as ready as he thought I was, because I can't stop freezing up around him like a smitten moron. I'm sure he's used to it, but...embarrassing.

I appreciate that he wants to teach me self-defense, and yeah, he told me that he's a teacher, but I'd rather be in a classroom with a professional than here in this rural torture chamber. I'm getting what I want—Hunter's hands on me— but not in the way I want it. I'd like him to be ripping my clothes off, but instead he's doing a slow-mo attack scenario that gives me all the proximity but none of the pleasure.

Ugh.

Of course *I* would go out for a one-night stand and wind up stranded with the one guy I can't seduce into meaningless sex. Story of my life.

And here he is, moving agonizingly slowly. His arms finally wrap nearly all the way around me, his pinkies sliding along the exposed skin above the waistband of my pants where my shirt's ridden up.

"Okay," he says, his stubbly chin scraping across the curve of my neck. "The next few will be half-speed and half-strength, and then we'll go full-speed and full-strength. How's that?"

It's great, it's fine. I can totally handle it. "Sounds good," I lie.

Hunter cinches his arms securely around my mid-section, but not tight enough for me to feel like I can't get away. I do what he taught me: lower my center of gravity and make it as hard as possible for him to hold on. Even at half-strength, escaping proves to be more difficult than I anticipated, but I'm able to break free relatively quickly each time.

During what has to be the fifteenth run-through of this, I'm struggling against his arms, his biceps forming a tight band beneath my breasts. I'm gonna go insane if we keep doing this.

"At what point would I kick you...I mean, *my assailant,* in the balls to get away?" I want to learn when to strike a blow so this lesson can be over and I can go to the opposite side of whichever end of the cabin he's in.

"If you're struggling to get free and it's not working, and you think you can get an advantage by startling your assailant enough to loosen their grip, bring your foot back to kick their shins, their knees. Beat on their arms. Elbow them, whatever you need to do."

"And risk pissing them off," I say.

"You're struggling, you've already pissed them off. And they have you at that point, so don't worry about pissing them off and worry about getting away."

Hunter still has his hold on me, so I wrap my hands around his wrists just as I crouch as much as I can. I bend at my waist, putting as much pressure as I can on his hands, and I break myself free once again.

"That was easier than I thought it'd be," I taunt, even though it really wasn't.

Hunter's eyes widen, and he lets out a surprised laugh. "It can't be that easy," he says smugly. "You're sweating and I'm not."

Well, that pisses me off. "You're twice my size!"

"I'm taking it easy on you."

I want to wipe that mischievous smile right off his stupid, handsome face. I told him earlier that I was competitive, but that may have been an understatement. I know he's taking that knowledge and using it to goad me, but I don't care. I'm *livid* at the idea that he thinks I wouldn't be able to get away from him.

"Stop taking it easy on me then," I say, unable to hide just how frustrated and pissed off I am. "Give it to me full-speed. If you want me to learn how to fend off an attacker, then attack me like an attacker would. Anyone who's trying to get

61

something out of me isn't going to sneak up behind me and seductively slide his hands across my hips."

Hunter's eyes flash with something, and I ignore the heat that rises in my cheeks because I've revealed too much. I really need an outlet for this sexual frustration that's drowning me, and if I'm not going to get that from him in the way that I want it, I'll take it in the way that he's offering it.

He raises his eyebrow at me, clearly ready to accept the challenge.

I'm going to take him down if it's the last thing I do. Considering how big he is, it very well may be.

There's fire in Hunter's eyes. Maybe he likes the way I'm challenging him, maybe he doesn't. I can't quite read it.

"Are you sure you can handle it?" He licks his lips as they curl up into a sexy smirk.

Ugh, I hate him.

"I'm sure," I tell him, sounding a lot more confident than I feel. Panic wells up in my stomach, because I desperately want to win this, and I'm not entirely sure that I can. My mom always tells me to fake it till I make it, so I guess that's the best way to go about this situation.

Hunter moves so quickly I don't even have time to antici-pate it. He doesn't grab me from behind like he did previ-ously. He locks his arms around me from the front, smashing my face against his chest.

My heartbeat ratchets up a few notches, my fight-or-flight reflex kicking in. He really isn't taking it easy on me this time, not that I expected him to. Just…the difference between our trial runs and *this* is night-and-day.

I'm not in the position to lower my center of gravity like we've been practicing, but I flail against his chest—god, he smells good—until I'm at least able to turn myself around in his arms, gaining some leverage against his body. I crouch down and lift my legs, bent at the knees, so that it's a little less easy to hold me up. I elbow at his biceps, pressing my ass against his thighs to push his hands loose. His grip is so *tight*.

I wiggle as much as I can, and maybe that works in my favor because my lower back is basically rubbing against his dick. He's curled around me and breathing heavily. When I move a certain way his breaths stutters, and even though trying to turn him on into surrender is a very dangerous idea, I'm too competitive not to use his erection to my advantage. I move a little more just to get him distracted, then slam my heel into his foot.

His breath catches and he loses his grip, but he still has one arm wrapped around my waist. His hold is loose enough that I can turn in his arms, and I push against his chest, then wrap my legs around his waist to throw him off balance. It works a little too well, because we both fall to the floor.

Hunter brings his arms around my back to absorb some of the blow, and we wind up on the floor with him cradled between my legs. He's breathing hard, his face inches from mine. He looks angry and frustrated and aroused. It's gorgeous.

He leans in close, the tip of his nose brushing against mine. The air is charged—an electrical current running between us— and I feel like I did last night in the alley. He's gonna kiss me this time, though, I know it.

"Hayley," he whispers.

I close my eyes and wait for it.

"This isn't the way you want to end up, on your back with your attacker on top of you." He leans in close, then says, "I win."

He pushes up onto his feet and reaches out to help me up.

I hate him.

As if being a loser wasn't bad enough, I'm a *sexually frustrated* loser.

And I want him even more than I did before.

After a dinner full of awkward silences, and a clean-up session that involves quite a few more, Hunter and I sit in the living area, looking anywhere but at each other. I know Hunter probably didn't mean to take advantage of my attraction to him in order to embarrass me, but he did, and now I'm stuck here with nowhere to go and nothing to do.

Restless, I move from the table and sit on the bed, plopping myself down on my back so I can stare up at the ceiling. The sun is setting, casting a gorgeous glow through the windows. It's beautiful here, but so *boring*.

Luckily—or *unluckily*, depending on how this goes—my need to break the silence trumps my lingering embarrassment.

"What do you do when you come down here? The entertainment options are...limited," I say, trying to be as charitable as possible.

"Sit outside in front of a fire," he says. The chair he's sitting in creaks as he shifts on it. "Read. Do some carpentry here and there. I come down here to give my mind a rest, so I don't have a TV or any movies. I don't bring my laptop. There wouldn't be much point to making the drive if I was going to do the same things here that I do at home."

"May I make a suggestion?"

"Sure," Hunter replies with a soft chuckle.

"Next time bring down a full deck of cards. And a board game, just in case."

"Noted."

"What do you read?"

"What?" he asks.

"You said you read," I explain. "What do you read? I don't see any books here."

"I bring one with me," he replies, like it's the most obvious answer in the world.

Surely he didn't bring one with him this time. "Do you have any games on your phone?" I ask, desperate.

"Nope. It's a burner."

"Ugh," I say dramatically as I flop my arm on the bed. "We can't even play Truth or Dare. There are only so many dares we could do in here all alone." *That* comment makes my mind go to some very pleasant and yet disappointing places, because think of all the sexy dares we could get up to if only Hunter was into me. Sometimes I think maybe…but if he was interested he would've said something when I mentioned the flirting in the club last night being real on my part, but he didn't. Ugh, what a waste of alone time with a hot, wonderful guy. "We'd have to play Truth or Truth."

"Okay, let's."

That gets my attention. I lift up my head to see what's going on over there. "You sure?"

He nods. "Absolutely."

"Any questions off limits?" I ask, rolling onto my side so I can get a good look at him.

"Not for me," he replies. "You?"

"No. Although rapid-fire questions make my brain-to-mouth filter go completely haywire, so there's no telling what you're in for right now."

"I think I can handle it," Hunter says. "Unless you can't."

"Ahhh, challenging me does actually work, as you found out earlier, so yes. Let's go."

"Favorite ice cream flavor," he asks.

"Starting with a softball to get my guard down? I like your style," I tease. "Vanilla."

"Vanilla?" he asks, surprised.

"Yep. A good vanilla with the flecks from the beans in it."

"It's so…"

"It's so plain, I know. But you have some vanilla in your freezer, and you want M&Ms in there? Put 'em in there. You want strawberries, put some strawberries in there. Coffee? Go for it. The ice cream world is your oyster with vanilla."

Hunter actually looks impressed with my answer. "I never would've thought of it that way."

"If you want to read into my personality with that answer, it's that I like to be in control." I say, waggling my eyebrows. "My turn?"

"Go for it," Hunter answers with a smile.

I'm in a dangerous mood and feel like playing with fire. "Weirdest place you've had sex."

His eyes widen only slightly in surprise before he says, "On a volcano."

"Oh wow." That was pretty much the last answer I was expecting. "How?"

"Well, when a man is attracted to a woman, he—"

"Don't be a smartass!" I say, slightly annoyed. "I wasn't asking about logistics."

"I was on a job in Hawaii, and we were on a hike. We just slipped off the trail behind a rock and…"

"You slept with a client?"

"No," Hunter replies vehemently, shaking his head. "I have not and would not ever do that. It was with someone who worked at the same firm I did, years ago. Things between us got…messy. That's one of the reasons I left, and that is definitely something I wouldn't do again."

"Was it fun?"

"The sex was good, and the fact that we could've gotten caught made it better. Never done it in public?"

"Me? No. I'm not opposed to it or anything, I've just never had the opportunity. I've also never been to Hawaii, but the possibility of volcano sex makes it appealing in a way it wasn't before."

Hunter laughs. "Did that count as a question, or do I get to ask you one now?"

I tap my finger on my chin, pretending to think long and hard. "I'll accept it as a follow-up within the context of my original question. Shoot."

He presses his lips together, then asks, "That message that Alexa asked that we pass on to you. She said she hoped you found what you were looking for last night. Did you?"

So...definitely *not* a softball question. I struggle with how much I want to tell him. There are only so many reasons I could make up for being in a club, and Hunter seems like the type who would see through a lie. Plus, after the things I said to him last night before I knew why he was really there, it's not like I could really deny what I was after.

"Alexa pretty much dragged me out to the club last night because she was worried about me becoming a shut-in," I tell him. "After Carson, I've had trouble trusting people in general, but especially when it comes to dating. I've been going through a bit of a dry spell, and she was starting to worry that I was becoming too attached to Netflix. So she basically stole my remote and sat on the end of my bed harassing me until I relented."

"So you wanted to meet new people?" His question is tinged with a teasing disbelief, because I know that he knows that's not what I was looking for. So I decide to give him what he wants.

"I wanted to have a one-night stand," I admit. "Just some good, old-fashioned, no-strings-attached sex. But you knew that already."

Hunter swallows, then shifts in his seat. "I did, yes."

"I left the club with a man, all right. But not in the way I intended."

"Life's surprising that way, isn't it?" he says with a laugh.

"I'm learning it can be, yeah. Ever been in love?" I ask.

"Once, yes," he replies with a sigh. "When I was young and stupid and didn't know how to handle it. It was...messy."

I let out a bitter laugh. "I know all about messy."

"Yeah," Hunter says sympathetically. "I guess you do."

"Me and Carson? We were a real shitshow."

Hunter runs his hand over his face, scratching at the stubble on his beard. "Do you mind... Is it okay if I ask what happened there? You don't have to tell me if you don't want to, I'm just curious."

I smile at him. "I think you have as much a right to know as anyone, considering the situation we're in."

"Still," Hunter replies solemnly, "you don't owe me an explanation."

Like hell I don't. It's nice that he's willing to give me an out, but I'm not going to take it.

"He was cute and charismatic. Something about him drew me in. My friends liked him at first, but slowly started to figure out that things weren't right with him. They warned me, and I didn't listen."

"It's hard to see when you don't want to see it," he says.

I nod. It's nice to talk to someone who has experience with getting all wrapped up in someone else's addiction. "Alexa told me he was manipulating me, but...I thought I saw a side of him that no one else saw, but really it was the other way around. Everyone in my life could see who he was, but I couldn't. When they tried to get me to open my eyes, I fought them every step of the way, and when he started showing me his true colors, I didn't want to believe it. And then...I was ashamed of myself for being so easily duped."

Just thinking about that time in my life—which I try so hard not to do—makes me want to cry.

"He stole my rent money once, and I told my parents I

had car trouble so they'd give me the cash to make up for it. He wasn't good for me, and I wasn't a good person around him. And all that is still following me around," I say, looking around at the cabin.

"I'm sorry," Hunter says.

"What do you have to be sorry for?" I say with a disbelieving laugh.

"I'm sorry that all that happened to you."

"It didn't happen to me," I admit. "They were all consequences of choices I made at the time."

"Hayley," Hunter says. "You shouldn't still be paying for that mistake."

"Maybe. If I wasn't here, Carson probably still would've managed to get *someone* wrapped up in this mess, and I wouldn't wish this on anyone. So maybe it's better it's me, because I have you."

I aim for lighthearted, but the compliment doesn't land that way.

"Yeah," he whispers with a hint of a smile.

"Can we talk about something else now?"

Hunter sits up straight in his chair. "Yes, absolutely. Uh… let's see…if you could have any job in the world, what would it be?"

I don't even have to think about the answer, I know it right off the top of my head. "You might think this is lame, but I don't care. I really want to be a financial planner. I want to have my own firm, be my own boss in charge of my own clients."

"Nothing lame about that," Hunter replies with a smile. "Being your own boss is great. Not having to answer to anyone, being able to take my business in the direction I want to take it in without having to consult with anyone or get anyone's approval is amazing. Why would you think I'd think it was lame?"

I shrug. "Just...having someone basically offer you the world on a platter and ask you what you'd pick? Saying you'd choose financial planning seems a little...safe."

"Who cares if it's safe if it's what you really want to do?"

"Also, I'd be amazing at it."

"So," he says, leaning forward and resting his elbows on the table. "What are you doing to make it happen?"

"I'm an accountant at the moment. I got a job with a good firm, and I have a mentor. I'd like to get some experience in different areas before I try moving up. I'm interviewing with a potential mentor next month. I'm hoping she can help me climb my way up the corporate ladder."

"A solid start," he tells me.

"Where are you from?"

"Richmond," he says. "My mom still lives there. My dad's in Denver."

"Oh," I breathe. "I didn't mean to—"

"It's okay," he assures me. "You couldn't have known. They got divorced after my brother died."

I nod sympathetically. My parents are still together, but I imagine the death of a child is a tough thing for a marriage to endure no matter how strong it is.

"What about you? Where are you from?"

I narrow my eyes at him. "Don't you have a file on me that has all of this information in it?"

He honestly looks taken aback. "No. I knew some fundamentals about your relationship with Carson, and I found your address and had pictures of you for obvious reasons. That's the extent of it."

"Well," I reply, "I grew up in Chicago. "My dad's a biology teacher, and my mom's a pretty well-known interior designer. They still live there in the house I grew up in."

"Do you see them often?"

I shake my head. "Not really. Holidays, mostly. We aren't

super close. They just let me live my life and only step in when I'm making terrible life choices, which has only happened once or twice." The aftermath of which I'm living right now.

"Least favorite food?" I ask, desperate to change the subject.

"Celery. You?"

"Cucumbers. Yuck." I take a minute to think of another question. "Dream vacation location."

He hums as he thinks of an answer. "Bali."

I gasp. "Mine too!" I feel kinda ridiculous getting excited about something so random, but here we are.

Hunter laughs. "Seems like we have good taste."

"Have you had to protect many people you know?" He told me he's doing this job out of obligation to Carson; it makes me wonder how many other things he's done for the people in his life.

"Absolutely not," he replies quickly.

The sharpness in his voice surprises me. "Okay, wow."

"No, it's…" He shakes his head, seemingly realizing how he came off. "It's kind of like how doctors don't treat their own family members because their judgment gets clouded. It's easy to lose sight of rational thinking when a loved one is on the line. It's why I don't protect my friends or family, and why I don't date anyone I protect."

His look lingers, and the air feels thick in my lungs.

"I'm even too close to this situation," he admits. "A couple of my guys asked me if I wanted them to take over for me, but I need to see this through. Plus, this was supposed to be a non-violent mission—just remove you from harm's way, take care of the situation, and bring you back when the threat was clear. I wasn't anticipating the gunfire in the club. I wouldn't have felt as good about it if there'd been more of a physical threat."

"You would've had someone else guarding me if there was?"

Hunter nods. "Yes. I trust my people; any one of them could've kept you safe, but I wanted to be the one to do it."

"You mentioned violent missions," I say, twisting the hem of my shirt between my fingers. "Do you have a lot of those?" What I really want to know is how often he's in danger of being shot, even though I know it's probably best if he doesn't give me an answer.

Hunter takes his time to work out an answer. "I'm an excellent fighter, and an excellent shot, but I do whatever I can to keep myself out of situations where I have to do those things. I don't enjoy fighting with people, and I certainly don't enjoy shooting at them, but my clients' safety comes first. Sometimes we have to do difficult things. There are parts of this job that are difficult for people to reconcile themselves with. There are days when it might not be so easy to look at yourself in the mirror."

I'm a little confused by the sentiment. "Criminals are criminals. If someone's threatening to harm another person, they should be stopped."

Hunter gives me a sad smile. "Criminals are human beings," he says. "You can't lose sight of that in this job. There are a lot of things someone who does this for a living needs to learn how to balance."

He's such a compassionate, caring person, all wrapped up in this amazingly attractive, lethal shell. I'm fascinated by him. "How are you doing with that?"

"The balancing?" he asks, amused.

"Yeah."

After a long look, he says, "Some days better than others."

Hunter's phone rings, skittering across the table. He glances at the caller ID. "I need to get this," he tells me.

Saved by the bell.

CHAPTER
Eight

I wake up to Hayley mumbling in her sleep, restlessly shifting beneath the sheets. She's clearly having a nightmare, so I reach up and place my hand on her bicep, then give it a reassuring squeeze. I'm hoping I can rouse her slowly; waking her up to unfamiliar surroundings seems like a bad idea. It'll be better if I can ease her out of this.

I flip on the lamp, just so she'll be able to see where she is when she opens her eyes.

"Hayley," I say soothingly. It's loud enough for her to hear me but not startle her awake. "It's okay, you're safe."

She bolts upright with a deep, panicked breath, pressing

the heel of her hand against her chest as she sucks in air like she can't get enough of it.

I lift myself up onto the bed and sit next to her, then slide my hand up and down her spine. She's shaking, clearly terrified from her dream, so I pull her close and offer what little comfort I can.

"Here," I tell her. I take her trembling hand and place it on the center of my chest, right over my heart so she can feel the steady beating. "Breathe with me. Slow and easy. You're okay, you're safe."

She does her best to match my breathing pattern as my chest rises and falls. It takes a minute or two for her breath to stop stuttering, but she manages. She slowly comes back to herself, and the panic ebbs away, taking the trembling along with it.

"Thank you." She drops her hand from my chest and places it in her lap. "I don't know what happened."

"Bad dream?"

"Not that I remember," she admits.

"You've been through a lot the past day and a half. The mind has weird ways of coping with that."

"Or not coping," she replies with a humorless laugh. "I just woke up terrified for no reason."

"Not for no reason." I rub a circuit along her spine, and her eyelids flutter closed. "You're sleeping in a strange bed, in a strange house, with a stranger."

"You're not a stranger. Not anymore." She gives me a smile that makes my damned heart skip a beat. She leans against me, her head resting on my shoulder. It feels…right in a way that I wish it didn't, because I'm having a hard enough time not kissing her as it is.

"Maybe we should get some sleep," I say, my voice more affected than I'd like.

She lifts her head, and she's so close I can feel her breathing. See the flecks of dark blue in her eyes. Smell the shampoo that she used tonight. It's mine, but it's different on her, makes me want to bury my face in her neck and breathe deep.

I'm *caught*.

I reach up and push a small piece of hair behind her ear, then slide the back of my knuckles across her soft cheek.

She's so gorgeous, even here with no makeup and her hair all wild from sleeping. I want her with an ache that seeps down into my bones.

I'm tired of not knowing what I'm missing, so I lean forward and kiss her. Hayley sinks into me, sliding her hand into my hair, pulling me close. She tastes like peppermint.

All too soon she's pulling away. "Hunter," she says, as the side of her nose brushes against mine. Her hands are fisted in my shirt, hanging on for dear life. "I don't know what—"

"I wasn't pretending," I tell her. This has to be confusing her, and I'm done sending mixed signals. I can't walk this back now, and I don't want to.

"What?" she says, pulling back, looking surprised.

"Last night you told me you thought I was pretending to flirt with you," I say, bringing her in close and kissing her again. "I wasn't pretending."

CHAPTER
Nine

I can't believe this is happening, but it is.

"In the club, when I saw you, I nearly blew it," Hunter says, cupping my face in his hands. "I wasn't thinking about why I was there, or keeping you safe. I saw you, and everything else disappeared. I was so attracted to you and *wanted* you more than I've ever wanted anyone in my life. It completely overtook everything to the point where I could've gotten you *killed*, Hayley. That's why I've been trying to stay away."

"But?"

He slides his thumbs across my cheekbones and gives me a smile that's so beautiful up close. "I can't do it anymore."

I have a long list of reasons why this isn't a good idea for me, either. We've only known each other for a day, but there's this underlying current of something *more* that I feel when I look at him, and it would be better for everyone involved if we just didn't go there. But my hormones are firing on all cylinders, and desire is thrumming through every cell in my body. I've wanted this since I saw him, consequences and aftermath be damned.

I lean forward and kiss Hunter's soft, soft lips. I memorize the noises he makes when I nip at his lip, when I sweep my tongue against his.

"This is probably a terrible idea," I say as I gather the hem of his T-shirt between my fingers and lift it up.

"Probably is," Hunter says. He's impatient; he reaches behind him, grabbing a fistful of collar and pulls it clean off, tossing it on the floor beside the bed.

Next he goes to work on my shirt, his fingers dancing across my skin and along my ribs as he slides it up, up, up. "We probably shouldn't do this," I say breathlessly and half-heartedly as Hunter gets me naked.

"Probably not," he says, licking his lips as he pulls the shirt over my head.

He zeroes in on my breasts, giving my nipples his full attention. He licks, sucks, and nips at them, taking his sweet time learning exactly what I like. Hunter is an incredibly quick study. A simple tug on his hair redirects him, and my moans and sighs have him doubling his efforts exactly where I want them.

I can't touch him enough; his skin is warm and smooth, and I want to put my hands everywhere on him. He shifts up onto the bed so he's kneeling, and he pulls me up along with him. I like this move; it gives us both better access.

He slips his hand into my panties, down between my legs, sliding his fingers against my wet flesh. I gasp, instinctively wrapping my arms around him before my knees give out. I rest my head against his shoulder as he slips his fingers inside, tightening my grip on him.

"That's it," he says in this low, filthy voice. "Hold on to me."

I do as he says, so turned on and keyed up that I don't even seem to have control of my own body anymore. Hunter thrusts his fingers, curling them enough to hit *just* the right spot as I rock against his hand. I move faster as the pleasure builds, practically mindless with it, when Hunter simultaneously pinches my nipple and sucks on that amazing spot just below my ear. I come with a rough shout, collapsing against Hunter as he holds me upright.

"Oh my god," I whisper, absentmindedly kissing his neck.

"Feel good?" he asks, as he runs his palm up and down my back.

"Felt amazing," I sigh. I press open-mouthed kisses across his collarbone, loving the soft noises he makes. I only stop when I hit a puckered patch of skin. I lean back to get a better look at him, and only then do I notice the scars smattered across his chest.

There aren't a lot, really, but enough that it's difficult not to notice.

I don't want him to feel self-conscious about it, so I reverently trace the mottled skin with my fingers.

"Hazard of the job," he says. But he looks a little unsure about what I think of them.

"I think they're gorgeous," I say honestly. They're physical symbols of the kind of man he is—the type of guy who puts his life on the line day after day.

"Yeah?"

I nod and kiss what looks like a bullet wound on his shoulder.

"I got shot," he says, voice raspy.

There's a long gash along his ribcage, a jagged wound with raised pink skin. I press my palm along the length of it. "A mugger tried to stab me."

I drag my lips along his shoulder, across his bicep as I move around to his back. There's a large patch of mottled skin just below his left shoulder blade. I lean in and press my lips against it.

"Clipped the pavement when I was taking a sharp turn on my bike," he says. "Wasn't wearing a jacket like I should have been."

I press my cheek against the scar and wrap my arms around his waist, holding him tight. He slides his hands across my arms until his hands are over mine, then he knits our fingers together. It's a nice interlude, a minute to hold each other, but I want to get back to all of the wonderful touching and kissing.

So I slide my arm down his abdomen, beneath the waistband of his pants. He isn't wearing any underwear, and that kicks up my pulse a few notches. With Hunter's hand still on mine, I grip his cock, giving him a gentle tug as I bring our hands up the shaft. Hunter moans, relaxing into me a bit, his back pressed against my chest.

"Show me how you want me to touch you," I whisper, skimming open-mouthed kisses beneath his shoulder blade.

His breath catches, but he does what I ask. He tightens his grip over mine as he guides me up and down. I move my other hand higher on his chest, just so I can hold on, and he brings our joined hands up to his lips, kissing my palm. His control is outstanding; I can tell I'm making him feel good by the way he tenses and relaxes, but he moves so slowly, like he's trying to draw this out.

"Hayley," he says, half whisper, half groan. His head lolls

back as I suck and lick his skin wherever I can reach. When I swipe a bead of precum with my thumb on a downstroke, the control I was admiring earlier completely snaps.

He sucks in a breath, releasing my hand and turning in my arms so we're facing each other, capturing my lips in a kiss that leaves me breathless. I lie back on the bed as he slides off my underwear, then lowers his body down onto mine. I'm lost in the scratch of his stubble as he kisses his way across my chest, then licks a stripe down my belly.

"C'mere," I say, impatient to have his mouth on mine again. He does as I ask, grinding his hips against mine, which makes me realize he still has way too many clothes on. I hook my toes on the waistband of his sweats and drag them down as far as I can. Hunter kicks his way out of them, smiling against my lips.

"I didn't want to stop kissing you," I say.

Hunter laughs. "I'm glad."

"We need condoms," I tell him. "I have some in my purse on the floor. Pull them out."

He does, then sits up on his knees as he rolls it on.

It's the first chance I've gotten to really admire just how amazing his body is. Broad chest, muscular thighs. He's gorgeous and aroused and grinning at me as he hastily rolls on the condom.

I crook my finger at him, and he comes eagerly, kissing me and then nuzzling my neck as he pushes inside. I close my eyes for just a second, taking a moment to adjust. The pressure inside me is *perfect*, and all I want is for him to *move*.

I cup his face in my hands, bringing him down for a long, slow kiss as he rocks with short, rhythmic strokes. He balances his weight on one elbow and explores my body with his free hand. He brushes the underside of my breast, gets a tight grip on my ass, then uses his thumb to rub maddening circles on my clit.

He latches on to that place on my neck that makes all my bells and whistles go off, and I give his hair a gentle tug every few strokes, because the short grunts that follow let me know he likes it.

"You feel so good," he says, sliding his hand up my thigh where it's wrapped around his waist.

He shifts us just a little bit, raising my hips so he can go deeper, his thrusts growing faster. That, along with the maddeningly perfect way he's playing with my clit, makes me come almost immediately, my hips bucking up to get all the friction I can as I cry out.

Hunter pulls away from my neck as I ride out my orgasm, his eyes shut tight, his face tense with pleasure. Now that I've had *two* amazing, mind-blowing orgasms courtesy of him, all I want to do is return the favor. With all my focus on Hunter, I slide my fingers into his hair and rock my hips, driving him closer and closer to the edge, his frantic breaths hot against my skin where he's buried his face into my neck.

"C'mon," I whisper, then take his earlobe between my teeth and tug.

His body tenses with a long, low groan as his hips stutter against mine, completely losing all his rhythm. He drapes himself on me like a hot, sweaty blanket, and the weight is nice. I lightly scratch my nails up and down his back as Hunter lets out long, contented hums.

He rolls away from me too soon, bending down to give me a sweet kiss before he goes into the bathroom to clean up.

When he returns, he crawls into bed and wraps me up tight.

"We're good at that," I say with a smile, running my hand up and down his arm.

He grins, then plants a kiss on my forehead. "We're great at that."

———————

Hunter and I doze on and off.

Around midnight I wake up to Hunter spooning me, kissing his way along the nape of my neck. I snuggle into him with a grin, wiggling my ass against his growing erection. He lets out a strangled noise, then says, "You're awake."

"I'm awake. How could I not be?"

He smiles against my skin, and I turn in his arms, anxious for his kisses.

He does not disappoint, melting against me as his tongue sweeps into my mouth.

We get carried away pretty quickly. "Ready for more?" he asks, teasing the edge of my earlobe with his tongue.

"Mmm-hmm." I reach back for the condoms on the nightstand, dangling them in front of Hunter's face. "It'd be a shame for these to go to waste."

He laughs. "How much sex were you planning on having last night?"

I hook my leg around his waist, using everything I have in me to roll him on his back. His eyes are wide with surprise, then hooded with desire. I grind down on his cock, and he rests his hands on my hips, guiding my motions.

The condom packet rips easily between my teeth, and Hunter looks like he's going to come out of his skin with desire when I roll it on.

I position him right where I want him, then sink down slowly. Hunter surges up, then kisses me fiercely.

"Guess you're just gonna have to find out."

———————

I wake up surrounded by Hunter. His smell is on the sheets, his warm body is wrapped around me, making me feel safer than I have in a long, long time. The room is filled with the cool gray light that hits just before the sun peeks over the horizon. One hand is tucked under my pillow, and the other slides down Hunter's arm, which is casually slung over my waist. He's rubbing lazy circles with his thumb just below my belly button.

It's been so long since I've woken up with someone that I've pretty much forgotten how nice it can be. I'm smiling into my pillow, my skin still buzzing from all the orgasms I had last night. Even though I didn't sleep very long—Hunter made sure of that—I feel more rested than I have since I moved to D.C.

I don't want to think about what that means.

Out of the corner of my eye I catch a slight flicker of light and realize that Hunter's awake. I turn my head and see he has his head propped up on his elbow. He's super engaged in whatever it is he's looking at because it takes a while for him to notice that I'm looking at him.

"Good morning," he says with a warm smile as he leans forward and presses his lips against mine.

I don't even think about what I'm doing, I just melt into his kiss. I manage to turn toward him without losing that connection, and mold my body against his.

"Did I wake you?" he asks.

I shake my head. "No. Should you have?"

"I've been up for a while. Went outside for a little bit."

That gets my attention. He hadn't opened the door to this cabin since we first walked in the night before last. He was nervous about me even peeking out the window yesterday, and now he's walking around outside?

I sit up, propping my head on my elbow, mirroring his position.

"Outside?" I ask.

Hunter's already smiling, but his smile gets even bigger.

It's warm and brings out the dimple on his left cheek. I don't even know what he's smiling about, but I can't help but grin, too.

"What's going on?"

"It's over," he says proudly.

"What's over?" I ask dumbly, ignoring the hammering in my chest and the way my nerves are firing on all cylinders in anticipation of what he's going to say next.

"This, you being here. You don't have to worry about Damien Hunt or Carson or anything like what happened the other night happening again."

A bolt of horror shoots through me. "Is Carson…" I can't even say it.

Hunter's eyebrows furrow. "No. No, he's alive. He's going into rehab this morning."

I sigh with relief. Even though Carson put me through so much shit, I still want him to get better. "One of my guys called in a favor with Damien," he tells me.

"Must've been a big favor."

"It was. He did it mostly for me."

"Seems like you inspire a lot of loyalty in your employees," I reply, reaching up and sweeping a lock of hair off his forehead.

He lowers his head, and I can almost make out the embarrassed blush in his cheeks in the early morning light.

He put his life on the line for me—a perfect stranger—because of a responsibility he felt he had toward a troubled friend of his brother's. I'm glad that kind of responsibility is paid back to him ten-fold by the people who care about him.

"Carson's persona non grata with that group now, so…at least he has one less channel available to him if he decides to start using again."

"That's good," I say. I mean it, truly. "So…" I slide my

finger along the ridge of his jaw, his stubble scratching the tip of my finger. "I can go outside now?"

Hunter nods, smiling. "You can go *home* now."

Never in my life have I felt such excitement alongside such disappointment. This ordeal didn't last very long, just like Hunter promised. I get to go home and see Alexa and get back to my life as normal. I'm happy for those things, really. But I can't stop the wave of disappointment creeping in because I'm going to be leaving Hunter. Last night was it.

But...that's what I wanted, isn't it?

"Did you hear me?" Hunter asks, sliding his fingers through my hair. "I'm gonna take you home."

I plaster on a smile so fake it almost hurts and try to stop my voice from shaking. I'm being ridiculous, I know I am.

"I heard you," I tell him. "But I don't want to talk anymore right now." I kiss him long and slow, and Hunter rolls himself on top of me until he's resting in the cradle of my hips. "I want to do other stuff."

"Yeah?" he asks breathily. "Me too. I can think of a few things I'd like to do, actually."

He kisses his way down my chest, his hands sliding up across my ribs until he's cupping my breast, his thumb rubbing across my hardening nipple.

I know I shouldn't do this, shouldn't let myself toe this dangerous line. Hunter's going to drop me off at my apartment, and I'm not going to see him again. But we have until then to be together, and what's the matter with taking some pleasure where I can get it?

I let my fingertips dance along the ridges of his ridiculous abs as I suck on the spot on his neck that I learned last night makes him a little weak.

We have one condom left, might as well put it to good use. I pluck it off the nightstand, tear the foil between my teeth. Hunter distracts me from my mission, though, wrapping his mouth around my nipple and pulling it between his teeth, making me gasp.

I reach down between us to roll on the condom, giving him a little tug before I do. He moans, and the sound electrifies me. I'm becoming addicted to it, and that's a dangerous, *dangerous* thing.

CHAPTER
Ten

We don't drag ourselves out of bed until mid-morning. If I didn't know how Hayley felt about relationships, I'd think she was reluctant to leave, but…that could be my own desire poking through the reality of the situation.

I'm taking her home today. She was very clear she isn't looking for a relationship, and it would be a bad idea for me to get involved anyway.

I keep telling myself that on a loop. Over and over until it sinks in.

We take a quick shower together, and the memory of the water dripping across her naked skin is gonna play on repeat every time I come down here from now on.

Once we're dry, Hayley slides on a pair of jeans that are just this side of too tight and make it difficult for me to look at anything but the curve of her ass. Now that I know what it looks like out of those pants, how her skin tastes and feels beneath my fingers, I can't look away. I can't stop wanting.

I can't stop *touching*.

Hayley doesn't seem to mind. When I reach out for her, she leans into my touch. It feels like we're a couple.

But we're not.

I keep telling myself that on a loop. Over and over until it sinks in.

Hayley carefully folds her clothes and puts them back in the duffle I brought them in. "Should I…" She awkwardly nods at the bag. "I mean, they're not mine, so…"

"Keep them," I tell her. They belong to one of my employees; I have no right to give them away. But I just can't stand the thought of them on someone else's body after this weekend.

I do a cursory check of the cabin to make sure it's in order before we leave, the same thing I do every time I come down here for a long weekend. It's nice to fall into a routine when the rest of my life feels so out of order.

It won't be the same the next time I come down here for the weekend. Hayley won't be with me, but she'll be everywhere.

"You ready?" she asks. Her brows are furrowed, she looks a little worried. "You okay?" She and I haven't spent much time together, but she can already read me so well. It's unnerving. And it's ridiculous how quickly I've fallen for her.

"I'm ready."

She nods and reaches for the duffel. I quickly reach out and grab the handles from her.

"You gonna get that cooler?" she asks.

"Nah, I'll bring it back the next time I come down."

She opens the door, then turns around and gives the place one last look. She's been stuck here for the past day and a half, anxious to go home. But now that we're leaving, she almost looks wistful.

I feel wistful.

Hayley steps outside and closes her eyes. She lifts her head up so the sun is on her face, and she takes a deep breath, holding her arms out, basking in it.

"I never appreciated nature until I couldn't go out in it," she says with a little smile.

I should go and put this bag in the trunk of the car, but instead I just stand here staring at her.

"It's been a *day*," I tease.

She squints, looking in my direction. "I know, but it was a *really* long day. I guess that thing about wanting something only when you can't have it is pretty true."

"Am I gonna have to worry about you hiking, or falling off a cliff, or getting lost in the wilderness?"

Hayley stares at me, the smile slipping from her face. I wonder what I've said wrong.

"No," she says. "You don't have to worry about me."

I'm going to anyway, but I don't tell her that.

Hayley looks over at the car. "Wow. This is even more of a beater than I thought it was."

I'm surprised at the shape it's in, too. The car is a complete shit heap. I know Davis wouldn't have given me a getaway car that wasn't mechanically sound, but looking at it now, it seems like a total miracle this thing didn't fall apart in the middle of 95.

"This place is so beautiful," Hayley says as she looks out at the lake. "I kinda want to run off that pier and jump into the water."

I remember her telling me yesterday that she's never been swimming in a lake. The thought of her soaking wet in that white T-shirt makes me want to encourage her to do it.

"You'd freeze to death," I remind her, my conscience getting the better of me. Also, cold water seems like a good thing to think of right now.

"C'mon," I tell her, nodding toward the car. "I'll buy you breakfast before we head back."

She smiles and gets in the car.

I take Hayley to the Main Line Diner, a local greasy spoon that's been a favorite of my family's since my grandfather built the cabin. It's a small-town, friendly place where the staff knows my usual and the coffee's always fresh.

Lou, my favorite waitress, greets me with an excited smile. "Hunter," she coos, opening her arms wide for a hug. "I haven't seen you in a while, darlin'."

She's short and sweet, a round-faced woman with large red glasses that are too big for her face, and a bouffant that's straight out of the sixties. She's been around as long as I can remember.

"Hey, Lou," I reply, as she squeezes the life out of me.

Her eyes light up when she spots Hayley, a mischievous smile on her face.

"And who's this?" she asks, sizing Hayley up before she turns her attention back to me. "A girlfriend?"

I'm not sure what to say, but Hayley steps in and rescues me. "I'm Hayley Grey, a…friend of Hunter's."

We're not dating, and I don't know the right word to describe what we are—if we're anything—but the *friend* hurts to hear more than I thought it would, which surprises me. What I want is…

"Nice to meet you, Hayley," Lou replies with a raised brow. "*Friend* of Hunter's."

Hayley follows Lou to my usual booth, and I manage to catch her blush as she walks by.

We sit, and Lou hands Hayley a menu. I've ordered the same thing since I was twelve.

"What's good here?" Hayley asks.

"Everything," I reply unhelpfully.

The place is half full, and the jukebox flips over from one happy oldie to another. Spoons clink against cups as people stir cream and sugar into their coffee. An old friend of my grandfather's nods at me with a kind smile. I like coming here—the place is full of nostalgia and the best parts of my childhood—but can't stand the pity on people's faces when they ask how my mom and dad are doing these days, their eyes telling me everything their words can't.

I don't want to hear what a good boy my brother was, or how my grandfather would've been proud of the man I've become. I just wanted to come here and share some of my past with a woman I never expected to fall for, who I'm going to say goodbye to in a few agonizingly short hours.

The morning light shines in through the window next to us, highlighting the messy waves in Hayley's hair. She doesn't have any makeup on and still looks kind of sleepy, but here in this simple diner in the middle of nowhere, she's the most beautiful thing I've ever seen.

She looks up from the menu, catches me staring.

"What?" she asks, her lips curving up into a smile as she bites on her lip.

"You're gorgeous," I tell her. Maybe I shouldn't, but we only have a few more hours together, so why not?

She smiles, tucking her hair back behind her ear as she looks down at her menu. "Thank you," she says quietly.

Lou walks over and pours me a cup of coffee, then asks Hayley, "You want coffee, darlin'?"

She shakes her head, wrinkling her nose. "No, thank you. Orange juice, please?"

Lou nods. "You want a short stack, two orders of bacon," she says, looking at me. "Are you ready to order?"

"I'll have two fried eggs, toast and bacon," she says, folding her menu and handing it over. "Thank you."

Lou smiles at her warmly. "Comin' right up."

"You have a usual," Hayley says with a bright smile, like it's the cutest thing in the world. "You have a usual at this little diner full of senior citizens that plays Motown on the jukebox. I wouldn't have guessed that about you."

I'm intrigued. "What would you have guessed about me?"

She purses her lips. "Mmm...I would've guessed that you ate breakfast alone. Hard-boiled eggs and oatmeal or something else kinda tasteless and healthy to keep up all *that*," she replies, waving in my direction. I mean, I thought you looked good before I saw you naked, but yeah...all that is A-plus amazing, and I wouldn't have guessed you'd come to a place like this and eat so much saturated fat."

I'm smiling at her like a complete dumbass, but I can't help myself.

"Don't look at me like that," she says, all flustered.

"Like what?"

"Like you think I'm cute."

"I do think you're cute," I reply.

She rolls her eyes but doesn't stop smiling. "Is it okay that I mentioned we're friends?"

That question takes me by surprise. "Why wouldn't it be?"

Hayley shrugs. "I don't sleep with my friends, and well... after we leave here you're gonna drop me off, and we're..."

Not going to see each other anymore, is what she stops

herself from saying. I don't blame her—I've been stopping myself from thinking it all day.

"Yeah," I say, my voice rougher than I intend it to be.

Slowly, Hayley reaches for my hand, lacing our fingers together.

"I never said thank you," she tells me.

"For what?"

"For coming to that club. For bringing me here. For making sure I was safe. For teaching me how to protect myself. You took a really scary experience and made it—"

"Remote?" I reply, needing to break up the tension.

She laughs, then sees right through me and squeezes my hand. "Nice. *Amazing.* Hunter, I—"

"Here we go," Lou says with a cheery voice, setting our plates down in front of us. "You two let me know if you need anything, okay?"

I nod, not able to speak.

"Enjoy your breakfast," she says with a wink. "*Friends.*"

Hayley slides her hand back into her lap, and we eat in relative silence, making polite small talk now and then. She comments on the song playing, and I tell her a story about an old friend of my grandmother's I see shuffling down the sidewalk across the street.

Friday night seems like a lifetime ago, and yet I haven't had nearly enough time with Hayley. I want to know everything about her, could listen to her talk for hours. But she's clammed up now, maybe because she felt like she was on the verge of revealing too much.

I've been there many times this morning.

Maybe it's best like this, putting up walls that will make goodbye easier.

I ask for the check as soon as we're finished, telling Hayley we'd better leave if we want to beat the holiday traffic. When I pay, Lou sends us off with a knowing look and a bag full of donuts for the road.

———

Neither one of us says much of anything until we're about 45 miles outside of D.C. It's been an easy drive; we haven't hit much traffic. I'm grateful for that. The last thing I want is for this ride to be any longer than it needs to, for so many reasons.

We hit a snag just outside of Fredericksburg, slowing down to a near stop in a jam that looks like it goes on for at least a mile. After drumming my fingertips on the steering wheel trying to think of something easy to talk about and failing, we finally hit open road. Hayley reaches into the bag between us on the seat and pulls out a donut.

She takes a bite and moans.

I fidget in my seat, thinking of cold showers and old ladies and anything to get my body to settle down. The last thing I need is to be in a car with a hard-on for the girl who's the best sex of my life and also never wants to see me again.

"These are so good," Hayley says, her voice sexier than I'm sure she intends it to be.

"Told you," I tease.

She grins at me, kicks off her shoes, and puts her feet up on the dashboard. She leans back in her seat, relaxing like we're heading off on vacation somewhere and this isn't nearly the end of the line for us.

She closes her eyes, letting her head loll back against the headrest as she slowly licks the powdered sugar from her lips.

I let out a strangled grown that's drowned out by the rumbling of the engine.

If I didn't know better, I'd swear she's trying to kill me.

CHAPTER
Eleven

We pull up to the curb in front of my apartment, and the place looks just like it did the last time I saw it, but *so much* has changed.

Hunter gives me a long look before he turns off the car, then walks over and opens the door for me. I step out and try to breathe through the heavy weight on my chest that's slowly been making itself felt since we turned the corner onto my street. I don't know what to say, and Hunter must not either, because he pops the trunk, pulls out the duffel, and then awkwardly hands it to me.

I can't tell him that these clothes have too many memories attached to them and I don't want them. I also don't have the heart to give those memories away, so I take the bag from him and set it at my feet.

"If you—"

"I wanted to—"

We both start talking at the same time.

"You first," he says after letting out a long sigh.

"I said it back at the diner, but really...I cannot thank you enough for everything you did for me. Putting your life on the line, putting your life on hold for me, and opening up your home to me...there are no words, so I have to settle for thank you."

With a breathtaking smile, he says, "You're welcome." He reaches up and plays with a strand of my hair. "I'd do it again in a second."

That kind of sets the butterflies in my stomach out in full force.

"In my experience, things get hard once you get home after something like this. If you need someone to talk to, if you have a bad dream, or...whatever. Please call me." Hunter slips a card into my hand, his personal cell number scrawled across the back in his messy handwriting. I stare at it for a moment, so glad that he's given this to me and still wishing he hadn't. I won't be able to throw it away, and I don't think I'll be able to stop myself from using it at some point now that I have it.

I swallow past the lump in my throat and nod, then ignore my better judgment and surge up on my tiptoes and wrap my arms around him, burying my face in his neck.

He does the same, and we hold on tight for who knows how long. I feel safer in his arms than I've ever felt anywhere else, and the smell of his skin comforts me like nothing else ever has. My head is swimming, and the very last thing in the world I want to do is let go.

This—I know from experience—is where my judgment

starts to get cloudy and where I start ignoring warning sighs. Hunter isn't Carson. I *know* that.

He isn't going to steal my rent for drug money, he isn't going to pawn my GPS to get high.

He isn't Carson.

I know that.

But still…when he lets go, I can't make myself ask him to stay.

———

"Oh my god," Alexa says as she launches herself off the bottom step of the stairway that leads to the front door of my apartment building. She moves at lightning speed and puts her arms around me so tightly that it's difficult for me to breathe. I try to hold her back, but I can barely move. "Are you hurt? Are you okay?" She lets me go and steps back, appraising me for injuries. "Are you hurt?"

I smile at her. "I'm okay," I reply softly, gently gripping her forearms to ground her a bit.

"I've been so worried about you," she says, bringing me in for another hug before she takes my hands in hers. "I'm so sorry I nagged you to go out. I should've never pressured you, and your life is *your* life. Whatever you need to do, whatever you want to do, just do it, don't listen to me. If you want to lie in bed all day, watch Netflix, and never have sex again, I will fully support you. I'll even bring you snacks."

"I appreciate that," I reply with a laugh, although I can't help the heat that creeps up into my cheeks because Hunter is *right there* overhearing all this.

This Alexa is a far cry from the collected person I talked to on the phone yesterday, who was teasing me about my hot bodyguard. She was probably worried sick when I spoke to her but kept herself calm for me so I wouldn't freak out.

I look over at Hunter, who's grinning at us with a soft look in his eyes.

"Who are you?" Alexa asks, narrowing her eyes at him. I know my best friend, and she's going to be like an attack dog toward any unfamiliar males for the foreseeable future.

Hunter is unfazed. He steps forward and reaches out his hand. "My name is Hunter, I'm—"

Alexa launches herself into his arms, and from the looks of it she squeezes him even tighter than she squeezed me.

Hunter gives me this cute, helpless look over Alexa's shoulder as he pats her back. I can't help but smile, because the whole situation is adorable. Alexa is enthusiastic and fun, a fierce, loyal person who wants the best for her friends and counts anyone who is kind to those friends as part of her circle.

"Thank you for taking care of my girl," she tells him. "I always want her safe, so thank you for keeping her that way. And thank you for keeping *me* safe, too, since I know you're the one who sent Jesse."

Hunter's helplessness relaxes into a kind smile as he wraps his arm around Alexa, giving her a hug before he sets her down.

"You're very welcome," he replies. "How was Jesse?"

"Are you asking as his boss? Is this a performance review?" she teases.

"An informal one, sure. I like to make sure my people are worth keeping around," he teases back.

"He got me out of that club, which seems like it'd be the most important part. He brought me home, even cooked for me a few times. Wouldn't let me out of his sight until this morning."

Pride lights up Hunter's handsome face. "Good to know."

"You should give him a raise," Alexa says. "I think he's a keeper." She smiles in a way that lets me know there's more to this story and makes me wonder if I'm not the only one who's going to have a difficult time leaving this weekend behind me.

"Noted," Hunter replies.

"I ordered pizza," Alexa says. "I brought wine, too. We're gonna watch movies all night long and get a little drunk since we don't have to work tomorrow."

"Sounds like a plan," I tell her with a smile.

"I'm gonna get going," Hunter says.

The smile falls from my face, because I don't want him to leave yet. I'm just not sure what else I can say. Inviting him inside seems like a bad idea... If I don't want to say goodbye now, doing it after spending hours with him in my apartment will be ten times worse. Probably impossible.

Alexa looks between me and Hunter, and she's standing close enough that I can hear the quiet "oh" when she says it.

"I'm just gonna go inside," she says, hooking her thumbs in the direction of the door.

"Okay," I reply. She grins and then walks away.

Hunter watches her go, and when the front door closes, he says, "I'm glad you have a friend like her."

I haven't known Hunter long, but something about the sentiment touches me in a way that's unexpected.

"She's the best kind of friend to have. I hope you have one like her, too." After seeing how stressful his job must be and how much he looks out for other people, I want him to have someone he can decompress with.

Hunter starts to say something but catches himself. He moves a couple steps closer to me instead, so close I have to tilt my head to see him.

"Hayley," he whispers, his eyes full of *something* that makes him even more gorgeous than usual, which is a feat. He takes my hands in his, and I let out a soft sigh at the feel of his warm skin against mine. "I'm sorry for the circumstances under which it happened, but I'm so glad I met you. Spending time with you was…a *pleasure*." He slides the pad of his thumb across my knuckles as he says it, sending an electric shiver up my spine that fizzles out into my fingertips.

I want to push up on the tips of my toes and kiss him, just one more time. Grab on to his shirt and pull him close and not let go until I'm ready.

But I don't do any of that.

"Goodbye, Hayley," he says, bringing the back of my right hand to his lips.

I'm completely transfixed by him, unable to move, until a car horn blares somewhere down the street and makes me snap out of it.

"Bye," I whisper.

I step away from him, grab the duffel, and turn to go inside. I don't look back, but I feel Hunter's gaze on me as I walk away.

When I open my apartment door, Alexa's standing at the window. Watching Hunter drive away, I'm guessing.

"Want me to tell you which street he turned down? It might give us a clue about—"

"I don't want to know," I tell her. If I start thinking about where he lives, then I'll do something with the phone number that's burning a hole in my pocket.

She nods, facing me after she tucks the curtain back into place. "How are you really?"

I drop the bag on the floor and shrug. "I don't know."

"Is it about what happened at the club?"

"No," I tell her right away. "I don't know. I think I'm okay? I'm not scared to be here, even though I thought I would be. I feel…fine."

"That's good," Alexa assures me with a smile.

"Are *you* okay? I'm sorry that you got dragged into this. If you'd gotten hurt, I—"

"Hey, hey," she says soothingly as she walks over and hugs me. "I'm fine. I got an excuse to spend the weekend at home with a hot guy—total ten—cooking me breakfast. No one got hurt, and you're here safe. What more could I ask for?"

"Carson's in rehab," I tell her. She hates his guts, but I tell her anyway.

"Jesse told me. I…might've ranted about Carson a little."

I laugh. Alexa's little is a lot.

"Do you want to talk about what I saw down there?"

I take a deep breath. I could tell that there was more to her time with Jesse than she let on, of course she'd catch on to this. I shake my head. I don't even want to *think* about what she saw down there. It's a lot, it feels…*important*, and I'm scared to get her take on things. Because she'd encourage me to go for it, or to leave it alone? I have no idea.

"Okay," she murmurs. "How 'bout I pick the wine, and you pick the movie?"

Sounds like a plan to me.

I lie awake the first night I'm home, mostly because Alexa and I stay up really late. Wine tends to keep me up all night, and I drank a *lot* of it. Plus, there's a part of me that's scared that if I go to sleep I'll have another nightmare, and there isn't anyone next to me who'll be able to pull me out of it.

Alexa is sleeping on my couch—she insisted—and it's nicer than being here alone. Even though I lie in bed willing it to come, sleep is elusive.

It's better when I get back into my routine. I take the Metro to work like I always do, and my coworkers are gathered around talking about the draft party for this year's fantasy football league. They ask me how my holiday was, and I spin a tale about taking a trip to the beach with some college friends who were in town.

No one suspects that this weekend my whole world was turned upside down.

Alexa keeps tabs on me from a respectable distance, doing her best to make sure I'm not alone if I don't want to be. She invites me out to dinner every night, and I go, but on the fourth night I tell her that she doesn't have to worry about me. That I think the sooner life goes back to normal, the better off I'll be. She seems skeptical, but agrees.

My nights are mainly nightmare-free, even though I'm still not sleeping well. I have a lot on my mind. The first major challenge I have is when a car backfires outside my window, and I wake up in a cold sweat, my heart pounding its way through my ribcage. I think about calling Hunter as I sit on the edge of my bed, counting my breaths, trying to calm down. I've been through a lot. Even though everything turned out okay, it would be nice to have someone tell me that I'm not being ridiculous when my pulse picks up if someone in a crowd looks at me too long, or when the rush-hour crowds on the train make me feel uneasy because I don't have an escape route to get out of there if I need to.

I know I can tell Alexa, but I don't want her to feel like she has to babysit me. I just want some reassurance, and I know Hunter could give that to me.

I start getting off the Metro a few stops before my usual one on my way home from work, exploring the city I haven't taken the time to get to know since I moved here. My bed doesn't hold the same allure that it used to, and I can't find anything I'm interested in watching on Netflix. I go out for walks in the evening, passing through the small boutiques nearby. I stay on busy roads and near crowds. I'm doing all right.

It isn't until I walk down the street that the club is on that

I let myself think about the night we first met, how much I loved the smell of his jacket, the warmth of his body by my side. I'm tired of pretending like there wasn't something there between us, like I'm not desperate to have it again.

Truth is, I'm lonely.

If I'm honest with myself, I have been for a long time. I crave companionship, someone to hold me when I lie in bed at night, someone to listen to me when I need to vent. That's not something that I can find with a one-night stand. I'd been foolish trying to convince myself that I don't want or need it. Alexa teased me about my produce-section fantasy man, but I think maybe he's a reality.

And I have his phone number at home in my bedroom.

That night, when I'm home, I slide the duffel bag across the room from the corner I'd stashed it in and plop on the edge of my bed.

I unzip it, hoping that maybe the clothes still smell like him. Pathetic, I know.

The first thing I see is Hunter's leather jacket, folded-up neatly on top of the stack. It's the one he put over my shoulders that Friday night that seems so long ago. I slide it on and press my nose into the collar, breathing in deep.

Exhausted and warm, I crawl up and collapse on top of my pillows, exhaustion finally pulling me under into a deep, deep sleep.

I wake up to the soft scratch of fingernails soothingly sliding across my scalp. For a second, I think I might be stuck in a dream, but my dreams have never quite managed to capture the smell of freshly brewed coffee. No, this is happening, and I am awake, and someone is making coffee in my apartment.

My eyes open to Alexa sitting on the edge of my bed,

giving me a fond smile as she brushes my hair away from my face. Sunlight is streaming through my windows, and I can tell by the light in my room that I've slept much later than I usually do.

I'm so groggy and confused that I can't think of anything to say to her other than… "What?"

"We were supposed to have our normal Friday dinner last night," she says, her voice calm and low. "You said you wanted to go back to normal, and that was our normal. When I didn't hear from you, I got worried, and you weren't answering your phone. I got in late last night, but you were dead to the world, and I didn't have the heart to wake you up. I know you haven't been sleeping very well."

I rub my eyes, pushing the sleep away. "I'm sorry I scared you," I tell her. "I completely forgot."

"I figured," she replies with a soft laugh. With a weak tug at the collar of Hunter's jacket—which I'm still wearing—she asks, "Wanna talk about this?"

I look at her for a long while, at odds with myself. "I miss him," I admit. "Isn't that weird? I knew him for a grand total of two days, but…it felt like he was supposed to be a part of my life." I shake my head at myself, because I know this sounds totally nuts. "I always get so worried about getting wrapped up in another guy like I got wrapped up in Carson. I don't trust how I feel, I worry about ignoring warning signs because everything feels so good. That smitten stupidity. But it's not going away now, and…" I shrug. "I just miss him."

Alexa grins, her eyes bright. "It's not nuts," she replies. "It happens. You felt a connection with the guy, and if it's not going away maybe that's fate trying to tell you something."

Playfully, I roll my eyes. "You know I don't believe in fate."

She purses her lips together, looking a little exasperated with me. It's good natured, though. "Fine," she says with a dramatic wave. "It's your heart, your mind, your whatever trying to tell you something. If it was just hormones or smitten stupidity, it would've passed in the past couple weeks."

She's right, I know she's right. "So what do I do?"

Alexa takes a deep breath. "You're going to have to decide if taking a chance on him is worth it. You don't have to get married tomorrow." She laughs when I tense up. "But you can get to know him, go on some dates. Take it slow. If it's not right, then you move on, but at least you'll know instead of always wondering."

I don't want to live with that regret. "He would've taken a bullet for me," I tell her. "There isn't any part of me that thinks he could possibly be a bad guy."

"Then I think you have your answer."

CHAPTER
Twelve

The days are long.

I throw myself into my work, thinking if I can get into some kind of a groove, I can distract myself from the fact that Hayley hasn't called. I expected a wait, but I hadn't expected more than a few days' wait. Every evening I pick up my cell phone and think about calling her. Every evening I decide against it.

After what happened with Carson, she has commitment issues. I understand that, and I'm dealing. The last thing I want to do is pressure her, because if there's a chance at all for anything between us, I have to be able to give her some space.

I'm trying.

A week after I dropped her off at her apartment, I take a cab to Union Station and head up to New York City. I've been looking to expand the business into another major market, and I set up meetings with a few potential stakeholders. Everything goes well.

I meet a few college friends for beers at a trendy microbrewery in Brooklyn. It's been a while since we've seen each other, and we sit around shooting the shit, catching up on each other's lives. My buddy Jake's getting married, and our friend Kyle's gonna propose next week. I update them on the state of my business, and when they ask if there's anyone special, I tell them I'm not looking. It's a lie—there *is* someone special—but telling them that she isn't interested in talking to me only invites more questions.

We hit up a Yankees game before I come home on the early train the next morning. The morning air is brisk, so I tell the cab driver to let me out early and I'll walk the rest of the way. He pulls over, and I sling my bag over my shoulder. I make a stop at my favorite local cafe for an egg sandwich and a fresh cup of coffee to help wake me up.

Coffee in hand, I step out onto the sidewalk and catch sight of Hayley crossing the street. My breath catches. Do I run over and talk to her? She looks in my direction, and for a second I think she sees me, but the rush-hour crowd is heavy, and she keeps on walking.

We only live three blocks away from each other, something I never told her.

As I make my way to the office, I wonder how many times I passed her just like this before I knew who she was. How many times I've passed her since.

I walk by Hayley's building often when I run my day-to-day errands. I turn right down her street to get to the local market. Turn left to get my dry cleaning.

I never run into her.

Two weeks in and still no call.

It doesn't go unnoticed at work that I've been on edge lately, that I've got a lot on my mind. I'm distracted, distant. Sometimes I snap even though I don't mean to.

One of my guys—Jesse—catches me in a particularly bad mood after a rough meeting with a potential client.

"Wanna go punch it out?" he asks.

Sparring sounds good; it'll give me a physical outlet to work out some of this frustration I've been carrying around with me.

"You sure? I put you on your ass three times the last time we sparred."

He replies with a cocky smile I want to knock off his face. "I'm sure. I've been planning my revenge. Meet you on the mats in twenty?"

I nod. "I'll be there."

Jesse kicks my ass.

He throws me off my game from the get-go, able to get in a few easy punches and a couple of kicks to my side. He clips me on the side of my chin, then sends me down on the mat with a leg sweep that I never saw coming.

That's when he calls a stop to things.

"Are you firing me or something?" he asks, tossing a towel in my direction.

I sit up, rest my elbows on my knees, and wipe the sweat off my face. "What?"

"Are you firing me? Is that why you're letting me kick your ass? You're off your game, and this seems like a pity fight. That's not you, so is this compensation for letting me go or something? What's going on?"

I sigh, running the towel along the back of my neck. "Nothing's going on." We're friends, I suppose, but he's not the guy I'd spill my guts to.

"Did something happen on the Grey case?"

I train my guys to be perceptive, but I don't enjoy that perceptiveness being turned around on me.

"What makes you think that?"

"No offense," Jesse says, looking over at me as he lowers himself to sit cross-legged on the floor. "But you've been hell to work for ever since then. I know you're close to the guy who caused her some trouble, but I thought he was in rehab? That's what Davis said, at least. Is that not going well or what?"

"It's not him," I say, tossing my towel on the floor.

"Then what...*oh*."

I don't even want to look at him; I hate that this is so easy to read on me.

"Yeah, oh."

"You gonna do something about it?"

"Date a client?" I say, testing the waters. We have a rule about dating clients; all my employees signed contracts stating they wouldn't. She's not my client anymore, but it'll be good to get a feel from Jesse for how the situation would go over with my employees. Provided I can ever get Hayley to call me.

Jesse rolls his eyes. "She's not your client anymore. No one here would bust your balls over it."

Good to know.

"I'm not sure she wants me to," I admit. Probably more than I should be telling him, but I can't deny that it's nice to have someone to talk to about this.

"I've worked with you long enough to know that you wouldn't be holding on to it if you didn't think there was something there. You're pretty good at cutting your losses."

"Yeah." He's right about that; I have a great feel for business and can tell right away when a situation isn't going to pan out the way I want it to. I'm not sure how well that ability transfers over to relationships, though.

"Alexa was pretty broken up over the whole thing," he tells me.

"Alexa?"

Jesse's eyebrows knit together. "Her friend?"

Oh shit. Yes, Alexa. "Right, right."

"She blamed herself for the whole thing, and got to talking. One thing she told me was that she thought Hayley was lonely but afraid to do anything about it because of everything that had happened to her. So keep that in mind," he says as he stands up. He walks over to the towel rack and grabs one for himself.

"Sometimes clients stick with you," he says, slinging his towel over his shoulder with a smile. "They stick. You should probably do something about it."

I hate to admit it, but he's right.

On my way home from the office, I stop by Hayley's apartment. I knock on the door and wait for a couple of minutes, but there's no answer. I consider waiting for her, but I don't want to be that guy; I think that might scare her off.

I take the steps down to the lobby and catch her walking past as I open the stairwell door. Without thinking, I reach out for her, sliding my hand along the inside of her arm.

She hauls off and punches me, putting her whole body into it. Pain blooms across my cheek, radiating out through my eye socket.

"Oh my god, Hunter!" she says with wide, panicked eyes. She reaches up and touches my face tenderly. "I'm so sorry, oh my god, I felt you touch me and I just reacted."

"It was a great punch," I tell her. "I taught you well."

"Are you okay? Come up to my apartment, let me get you some ice." She takes my hand and leads me to the elevator.

This isn't how I thought this evening would go, and even though I'm gonna have a hell of a shiner, I'm feeling no pain.

CHAPTER
Thirteen

"Will you sit down? Stop pacing," Hunter says patiently from where he's sprawled out on my couch holding a bag of frozen baby peas against his rapidly swelling cheekbone.

"I can't stop pacing," I argue. "Look at you! Look at what I did to your insanely gorgeous, unbelievably hazel eye!"

"It's fine," he tells me with a warm smile, looking at me in a way that's too amused for the situation we're in. He's so gorgeous, even with a bag of frozen produce resting on his face. It kinda makes me hate him a little. "I've had worse, Hayley."

"So? Is that supposed to make me feel better?" I say, my words laced with rapidly rising panic. "I don't want to be the person who gave you something that you can compare to your 'worse' injuries. What kind of story is that?"

"We met at a club where people were *shooting at you*. It's exactly our kind of story."

That gets a smile out of me. He has a point.

"This is my fault," he begins, but I'm not about to let him finish that sentence.

"I'm the one who—"

"I was stupid and put my hands on you when you weren't expecting it, and you did exactly what I taught you to do. It was amazing. This doesn't bother me, so it shouldn't bother you."

I let out a low groan, because even though he's trying to let me off the hook, I can't let myself off the hook.

"What can I do to make it better?" I ask.

He returns the question with a mischievous grin. "You can kiss it better if you want to."

I blush, but the corners of my lips lift up into a half smile.

"Come here, please."

I do as he says and sit next to him on the couch.

"It still hurts," he teases. "I think you need to get a little closer."

I let out a huff of a laugh, because he's pretty smooth when he wants to be. I move toward him, and impatient man that he is, he reaches out and slides his arm around my waist, tucking me into his side.

"Is that better?" I ask.

He nods, with a shit-eating grin on his face. "Much." He turns his head and presses a kiss into my hair.

"I was going to call you tonight," I admit. "I've wanted to call you for a few days now."

"Why didn't you?" he asks. There's no judgment, only curiosity. "I've wanted you to call me ever since I dropped you off, but I didn't want to pressure you, and I didn't want you to feel like you had to jump into anything you weren't ready for. It killed me to drive away that day."

"Why were you here tonight?"

He laughs. "I got tired of waiting."

"I didn't call you because I wasn't ready. Then the other night, I found your jacket in that duffel bag of clothes you gave me. I fell asleep in it, and Alexa found me the next morning. We had a chat about you, and she helped me see things more clearly."

"Why did you sleep in my jacket?" he asks, taking my hand. "Are you still having nightmares?"

"No, just one. I didn't mean to fall asleep in it, but I did put it on." I look down at my hands, preemptively embarrassed about what I'm going to say next. "I like the way you smell. It smells like you."

Hunter pulls me close, rests his head on mine and takes a deep breath. "I've missed you."

"I've missed you, too. But that's insane, right? We knew each other for, like…forty-eight hours. That's nothing! We barely know each other, but in some ways I feel like I've known you forever."

He lifts his free hand and threads my fingers with his. "We definitely have a connection. I'm not trying to pressure you, but I want to be honest here. I want to see where this goes. Are you okay with that?"

I push past the rush of nerves and say, "Yeah. I'm okay with that."

"Good," he replies. "I don't want to spend the rest of my life wondering what would've happened if I'd walked you to your door that night instead of driving away."

"Maybe it's a good thing you didn't. It took me a while to come to terms with how I was feeling. Then? I might've panicked."

"If you start to get scared, let me know. We can work on that. But Hayley?"

"Yeah?"

Hunter puts the bag down and tilts my chin up so I'm looking him in the eye. "I'm not Carson. I'd never hurt you on purpose," he says solemnly, like a vow.

I place my hand on his cheek. "I know you wouldn't. I know that." I push myself up and give him a long, lingering kiss, the two of us just breathing each other in. "I've missed this," I tell him, then kiss him again, just because I can.

"Seems like we're off to a good start," he says, smiling.

"Except for the part where I gave you a black eye." Tenderly, I run my fingers across his swollen flesh, wishing I could heal this with my touch. Hunter doesn't flinch, just lets me do what I need to.

"If someone's gonna give me a black eye, I'd rather it be you." He's grinning like a fool, and our next kiss is a little too toothy, but I'm too happy to care. I'm taking a chance for the first time in a while, and it feels amazing.

Hunter leans back and takes a good look at my apartment. "This place looks like you."

"What does that mean?" I'm just happy I managed to keep the place clean for the past few days. It would've been mortifying if he'd come up and found my panties hanging on a doorknob or something.

"Light and sunny. You have a ton of books...I knew you would. There are pictures everywhere. It's friendly. It reminds me of you."

I can't think of a better way to have someone like Hunter describe me.

"Is it okay if I look around?" he asks.

"You let me look around your place, it's only fair if I return the favor."

I take the peas and drop them in the sink as Hunter looks

around my apartment. It's unnerving having someone examine my things like this; I admire Hunter for letting me do it when we'd only just met. He takes his time, reading the spines of my books, examining my photographs, reminding me to water my plants.

"You don't have a TV in here," he notices.

"I moved it into the bedroom during my sad binge-watching phase where Netflix was my boyfriend."

Hunter looks mock offended. "If we're gonna do this thing, you two have to break up."

"Already done. We broke up when I got back from the cabin, I just haven't gotten around to putting it back where it belongs."

"Where's your bedroom?" he asks.

I narrow my eyes at him. "Are you asking that because you want to move the television, or…"

He places his right hand on his chest. "I'm not trying to trick you into getting naked, promise. Unless you want to get naked. In that case I'm all for it. I won't ever turn down nakedness, by the way. That's something you should know about me."

"Good to know," I reply.

"But in this case, I'm offering to bring your TV out here and reconnect your cable."

I take his hand in mine. "C'mon."

CHAPTER
Fourteen

When I woke up this morning, I didn't think I'd end the day with a throbbing black eye and a very naked, very happy Hayley wrapped up in my arms. Her head is on my chest, her long hair fanned out across my bicep, and she's tracing lazy, nonsensical patterns along my ribcage.

I could stay just like this forever.

The television has been moved back to the living room where it belongs, because I plan on giving her all the entertainment she needs in here from now on, for as long as she'll have me.

"Is 'let me reconnect your cable' code for sex now?" she asks, before playfully dragging her lips across my chest.

"Hey," I reply with a laugh. "I did actually reconnect your cable."

"Three times." She looks up at me, her eyes heavy-lidded and her hair a sexy mess, and clearly a fan of euphemisms.

"You came three times? I only counted two." Next time I'll aim for four, but this time we were frantic and not too worried about taking our time.

"Mmmm." She nods, laying her head back down on my shoulder and sliding her warm hand around my waist. "There was a third one right after two."

I'm grinning even though I'm trying hard not to.

"You don't have to look so smug."

"Get used to it," I tell her, curling a strand of her hair around my index finger.

"Get used to what? Coming three times, or you being smug?"

"Both, because one will happen right after the other."

She laughs. It's gorgeous.

I turn my head and notice a frilly album propped up against her lamp on her nightstand. "What's that?"

"A photo album from the volleyball team in college."

"May I?"

She nods.

I flip through, anxious to get a glimpse of her life before I knew her. There are lots of shots of Hayley in action, diving for the ball, jumping into the net. Quite a few of her and her teammates traveling for competitions, hoisting up trophies on podiums. I'm especially interested in the pictures of her in her uniform.

I point at a photo and ask, "Do you still have these shorts?"

She laughs and rolls over, resting her chin on my chest. "Maybe, why? Are you into role playing?"

"I'm into you in this uniform," I say, sliding my hand down the small of her back, then lower. "It makes your ass look amazing. Not that it doesn't already."

"Good boyfriend answer," she replies. "Not that you didn't show ample appreciation for my ass earlier."

I laugh, but her eyes grow wide with panic. "Oh god, was that too soon?"

"Too soon for what?" I'm totally confused.

"I called you my boyfriend. Kinda. I implied that you're my boyfriend."

I smile, then pull her closer for a kiss. We get carried away for a while, and she pulls away from me before I'm ready for her to go.

"It's nice having you here," she says, relaxing against my side.

"It's nice being here." I slide my fingertips up and down her arms, enjoying the feel of her skin against mine. "I have a confession to make."

Hayley tenses, just for a second. "What is it?"

"I saw you walking down the street last week," I admit.

"You did?" She turns toward me and runs the backs of her fingers along my jawline. "Why didn't you say anything?"

"I was trying to give you your space. I actually walk by your building a lot. I live only about three blocks away from here."

"You do?" she asks, her eyes wide. "Since when?"

"I do." I give her a soft kiss. "It was my first apartment in D.C."

"Wow," she sighs. "That's convenient."

"Yeah, I look forward to making that walk frequently."

She grins and nuzzles into my neck. "Even though you don't have far to go, will you stay tonight?"

"Have you been having nightmares?"

She shakes her head. "No. I just sleep better with you than I do without you."

"Okay," I reply, reaching over and turning out the light. "I'll stay."

Epilogue

Hunter does this on purpose, I know he does. We've been together long enough that he knows what gets me going, knows just how to push my buttons.

I've been nagging him to paint the cabin for months now, and he waited until the hottest day of the year to do it, because he knows that seeing him in a sweaty white T-shirt just *does* things to me. He checked off this item on his to-do list just in time, because our wedding's in two weeks. Even for a small backyard ceremony, there's a lot we need to take care of.

"Here," I say, as I hand him a glass of iced tea. "I thought you could use this."

Hunter's sprawled out on a lawn chair in paint-spattered jeans and that damned T-shirt, looking good enough to eat. He grabs the hem of his shirt and wipes his face with it, which shouldn't be as hot as it is.

He takes the glass of tea in one hand, then wraps the other around my waist and pulls me onto his lap.

"Thanks," he says, nuzzling my neck with his still-sweaty head, which makes me squeal. He laughs against my neck— his warm breath cooling the sweat on my skin—and kisses me there.

"You need to take off this shirt or you're gonna get weird tan lines."

He looks down at it and shrugs. "What does it matter if I have weird tan lines? I'm going to be wearing a suit. And we're going to Bali on our honeymoon, which is a place where I plan on getting a tan. And not wearing a shirt." He moves his head just so slightly upward and sucks on that spot below my ear that drives me crazy. "I plan on not wearing much of anything, really."

"Mmmm," I hum dreamily, running my fingers through his damp hair. "Bali. It's really hot out here; you should come in soon. You can take a shower, and then I can help you get dirty again."

Hunter raises his brow, then gives me a smile. "I'm almost done."

"I wish we'd put central air on our wedding registry," I tease.

"The window unit acting up again?"

"Yeah. I just want to cool off."

"I think I know what will help," he says with a grin and a mischievous glint in his eye that I've learned by now is completely untrustworthy. He sets his glass of tea on the ground.

"What are you gonna do?"

Hunter moves quickly, wrapping me up in his arms and jumping out of the lawn chair. I trust him with my life, so I wrap my arms around his neck and laugh as he runs across the pier and flings us both into the water.

"You jerk!" I laugh when we surface. "This is my favorite shirt."

He looks so pleased with himself that I can't be mad at him, but I do splash him with a handful of water. Instead of flinching, he just grabs my hand and pulls me close until I can wrap my arms and legs around him.

"You love me," he says.

"Enough to marry you, I guess."

"I can't wait." He moves in for a kiss, but I can't stand the lake water, so I give him my cheek instead. "Is it too early for a wedding present?"

We've been down this road before. "I'm not having sex with you in this lake, I don't care if we're getting married or not."

Hunter laughs. "Not a present for *me*, a present for you."

"Oh." I perk up. "In that case it's never too early."

"I've been watching that movie you love."

I narrow my eyes. "Which one?"

"*Dirty Dancing*?"

"Okay," I reply, drawing out the word. I'm really not sure where he's going with this.

"Do you remember what you told me the first time you came down here?"

I close my eyes, pulling from the deep, dark recesses of my terrible memory and draw a blank. Which is distressing, because clearly whatever I said to him made enough of an impact for him to want to do something about it.

"You said you thought the lift was—"

"Peak romance!" I'm so excited I remembered that I cut him off.

"Right," he says, coming in for a kiss. This time I let him have one.

"I thought that was peak romance before I met *you*, babe. You left that in the dust a long time ago."

"You don't want to learn how to do the lift?"

It could be fun. A wet Hunter is always a good time. "Maybe after the wedding? I don't want you to throw your back out or something. We need that for very important things in the coming weeks."

Hunter gives me the dirtiest grin. "I have a *very* strong back."

"Mmmm-hmmm," I hum against his lips. "Very strong."

"Well," he sighs. "That was my plan for this afternoon. Now what do you want to do?"

"Take me inside," I tell him. "All I want is you."

Printed in Poland
by Amazon Fulfillment
Poland Sp. z o.o., Wrocław